PAXTON'S PROMISE

A GLOVES OFF NOVEL

NEW YORK TIMES & USA TODAY BESTSELLING AUTHOR

L.P. DOVER

Copyright © 2014 by L.P. Dover
Cover design by Regina Wamba of Mae I Design
Photo taken by: FuriousFotog
www.onefuriousfotog.com
Editing by Victoria Rae Schmitz, Crimson Tide Editorial
Formatting by JT Formatting

Printed in the United States of America
First Edition: November 2014
Library of Congress Cataloging-in-Publication Data
Dover, L.P.
   Paxton's Promise (A Gloves Off Novel) – 1st ed
     ISBN -13: 9780990396482
     ISBN -10: 0990396487

1.   Paxton's Promise—Fiction 2. Fiction—Romance
3.   Fiction—Contemporary Romance

http://**authorlpdoverbooks.com**

Gabriella

FOR THE PAST week, Paxton had given me time to adjust to my life without Ashleigh by my side. She was gone to her cabin in the mountains, living the dream life. I was happy for her and Ryley, but I sure as hell was going to miss her. I had a feeling I knew what Paxton's terms were going to be anyway. *Maybe he'll forget about me this week?* Fat chance on that.

When the knock sounded on my door, I knew it was either Bradley or Paxton. For the past week, I had basically thrown Bradley to the side, and I could feel the hole growing bigger between us. Every time I was busy, I was with my fighters and he didn't like it. We spent more time angry at each other than actually civilized. However, when I opened the door, it wasn't Bradley. It was a tattooed fighter wearing fuck me jeans and a tight black T-shirt.

Walk away, Gabby.

"So we meet again," he said simply. For a moment, his sea green eyes flustered me like they did every time I saw him. This time, I couldn't let that happen.

Throwing open the door, I rolled my eyes and ventured back into the living room. He was going to come in anyway, there was no reason to stop him. "It appears so," I grumbled. "I was wishing you'd forget about me. I guess the hundred pennies I threw in that well didn't work."

The door shut and I could hear him chuckle. "Sorry, love. No wish is going to get you out of our agreement. I gave you a week of freedom, but now your time's up. You're not thinking of backing out are you?" Instead of sitting beside me on the couch, he sat in the chair across from me, his gaze boring straight into mine.

"No. I made a promise and I'm going to keep it. I always keep my promises."

"And the same goes for me," he murmured, voice smooth and deep. "Now, how 'bout we get down to business?" My heart sped up at the thought and a small smirk splayed across his lips.

"Fine," I answered, clearing my throat. "I'm sure it's nothing I can't handle."

The deep chuckle in his chest rumbled all the way down to my clit. "Oh, we'll see about that, sunshine. First, I need to know. What's the status with you and the douchebag baseball player?"

I crossed my arms over my chest. "I don't think that's any of your business."

"It is now, considering for the next month you're going to be with me and me only. You're going to have to get rid of him."

My eyes went wide. "Are you serious? What am I supposed to tell him?"

Nonchalantly, he shrugged. "I don't give a shit what you tell him, as long as he knows to stay away from you. If he so much as causes a problem, I'm going to extend the month."

"Don't you think this is a bit extreme? Wouldn't a week suffice?"

His expression grew serious. "You obviously have no idea how far out I put my neck on the line for you. I think a month is being very generous."

After experiencing life in the Dark Side, I could see where he was coming from. Those people wouldn't think twice about putting a bullet in my head. In fact, I'd say their humanity was long gone . . . just like Camden's.

"Okay, fine," I gave in. "A month it is. You don't expect me to fuck you though, right? That shit's not going to happen."

Paxton tilted his head back and roared in laughter. "Oh, Gabby, as much as I'd love to have you spread out for my delight, I would never ask that of you. But if you wanted it, I'd be happy to oblige."

I scoffed. "Don't worry, I think my lady bits can withstand what you're offering. When does all of this start?"

"Tomorrow," he noted, getting to his feet. "I trust you'll handle everything with your boyfriend today?"

I stared at him in hopes he'd smile and tell me it was all a joke. Sadly, I didn't get that. "Yes," I sighed. "I'll talk to him."

He strolled to the door and I followed to make sure it shut behind him. Paxton opened it wide and stopped. His back was to me, but then he turned around, piercing me with his green eyes. "Good, then we won't have any problems. If he really wants you, he'll wait for you." He stepped closer and circled a strand of my midnight hair through his fingers, his voice dipping lower. "It won't matter though. I know you won't go back to him after I get done with you."

"Sorry to disappoint, but that's not going to happen either," I said, glaring at him.

"It wasn't a wish," he clarified. "It was a promise— and you know how I feel about those." He winked and disappeared out the door, his footsteps calm and collected as he descended the stairs.

Growling in frustration, I slammed the door and stormed back over to the couch. *Fuck him with twelve giant cocks.* He didn't know what the hell he was talking about. I was going to make damn sure that promise was a promise he couldn't keep. What an arrogant prick.

Closing my eyes, I leaned my head against the couch and sighed. Only one more day of freedom. How was I going to spend it? The answer came with a text.

Bradley: I need to talk to you. Can I come over?

Here we go. If there was ever a time we should split up, it would be now. There was no way he was going to put up with me being with another man for the next month.

Me: Sure. I have lots to tell you too.

And none of it was good. Quickly, I dialed Ashleigh's number. I needed her guidance. "Hey, Gabby, what's up?"

"I just talked to Paxton," I blurted out.

"And?"

"And I'm in some deep shit."

CHAPTER 1

Gabriella

I NEVER THOUGHT breaking up with someone could be so fucking difficult. I was sitting by the window with my legs bouncing up and down while I waited for Bradley to show up. Not only was I letting him go, but it would be the second time I'd done it to him. He deserved someone who could be there for him, which clearly wasn't me.

I jumped when my phone rang and almost fell out of my chair. Thankfully, the coffee table saved me, but when I looked down at my phone, I groaned. *Please don't tell me my brother needs me to train right now.* Fighting was fun, but he had a tendency to overdo it sometimes.

When we were younger, he was the one who took care of me and our mother because our father left when I was just a toddler. Ever since then, Matt had worked for our neighbors, cutting grass and doing odd jobs just to help my mother bring in more money. We lived on peanut butter and jelly sandwiches for a long time. It was crazy how things changed.

"Hey, Matt," I answered.

"Hey, what are you doing?"

Turning my head toward the window, I could see Bradley's blue truck pulling into the parking lot. "I'm waiting on Bradley. He just drove up."

The sound of my nephew laughing in the background made me smile. I couldn't wait to hold him again. And now there were two more babies coming into the mix, once Ashleigh and Ryley had their twins. If there was anyone I missed more than anything it would be them. They were my best friends and now they were gone to the mountains to raise their kids in peace. It just reminded me of how alone I was.

"Are you two going out tonight?" my brother asked.

I huffed. "Not exactly. So, what's going on with you? Do you need me to train today?"

"Actually, no. That's the reason I'm calling. Since you don't have any fights coming up for a while, I thought it'd be best for you to take some time off."

Eyes wide, I jumped out of my seat and squealed. "Are you serious? You're really going to let me take a break?"

He chuckled. "Damn, don't sound so surprised. I'm not a slave driver, Gabby." *That's what he thinks.* "But yes, you need some time off. Shelby and I are going to take the baby and go on a vacation for a few weeks. I think we all need it."

"I couldn't agree with you more," I remarked. "How

long of a break are we talking about?"

"I'm thinking six weeks. But I need you to promise to keep up with a workout routine and stay active."

He didn't have to worry about that. I was going to be with Paxton every day for the next month, and I was positive he would keep me busy. Luckily, my brother was going to be gone and not paying attention to what I was doing. Since none of us could talk about the Dark Side, my brother didn't know about my involvement in it; hence, the reason why he wouldn't understand my living with Pax. I had to hope and pray he didn't find out.

"I'll be fine, Matt," I promised. "I'll work out every single day and eat right. Well, except for my Ben and Jerry's. I simply can't live without it."

He chuckled and I could almost hear him rolling his eyes through the phone. Men would never understand a woman's need for ice cream and chocolate. "All right, but not too much of it." I couldn't promise that. "And just so you know, we're probably going to our house at Oak Island, but before we leave I'll give you a call. Make sure you swing by the salon and see mom. She said you haven't been by in a while."

"Yeah, well, it's been a hell of a week. If only you knew."

"I think it's best I didn't."

"Yes, we'll leave it at that. Have fun on vacation. Maybe one day I'll be able to go on vacation like that."

Both he and the baby laughed. "You're more than welcome to come with us. I think your nephew would agree." Bradley knocked on the door and it was so loud my brother could hear it through the phone. "I guess that's my cue. Oh, don't forget to call Garrett. He's been hounding me since you haven't been returning his calls. He needs an answer about the movie within the next week."

Yes, he does. Unfortunately, I didn't have an answer for him. I was being offered a role in a movie, and although the thought was exciting, I'd have to put my fighting on hold while the filming took place. Fighting was what I was good at and I didn't feel comfortable leaving it. Not to mention, I had no experience in acting. I didn't want to look like a fool.

"Don't worry. I'll call him . . . eventually."

"Just make sure you do. And while I'm gone, don't do anything stupid, you hear me?"

Getting up from my seat, I wiped my sweaty hands on my shorts and started for the door. "Gee, I love the encouragement, dear brother. Don't worry, I'll be fine. You just go and have a good time."

"Will do, sis. Take care of yourself."

"I always do."

After we hung up, I set my phone down on the kitchen counter and opened the door. My heart thumped so hard it made my chest hurt, especially when I got my first look at Bradley. His warm smile was the first thing I saw, followed by his gorgeous caramel colored eyes, which were almost hidden underneath his USC baseball cap.

Opening the door wider, I beckoned him inside. "Come on in."

He stepped through the threshold and took off his hat before running a hand through his chestnut brown hair. "Thanks," he said, setting his hat down beside my phone.

I started to walk into the living room, but then I noticed he wasn't following me. It was clear something was wrong. Turning to him, I confronted the silence. "What's up?"

He averted his gaze, licked his lips, and pressed them together.

Something was definitely not right, he wouldn't even look at me. "Bradley, what's going on?" In my heart, I already knew. I could feel it inside, with the way he looked at me when he walked through the door.

"I'm done, Gabby," he blurted out. "I've tried to do the whole friends with benefits thing, but it's not working." He'd reached his breaking point. But there was nothing I could do about it.

Hanging my head, I nodded. "You're right, it's not. So what exactly are you saying?"

"I think you know. I've tried to be patient in hopes you would really come back to me, but I was a fool to think you would. This is me bowing out and moving on. I can't play second best anymore."

My eyes burned as he spoke the truth. I had no choice but to agree with him. "I never wanted you to feel that way," I murmured, lifting my head.

Sighing, he moved closer and pulled me into his arms. "I know you didn't. Making you choose between me and your friends wasn't fair. Ever since that moment, I could feel the tension increasing between us. Things won't ever be the same and you know it."

"I know," I whispered, holding him tight. Burying my face in his chest, I breathed him in one last time. I knew after today I probably wouldn't see him again. In the end, breaking up would make my life easier, but knowing that still didn't help.

My heart ached for him, for the friendship I was losing. Bradley had been a part of my life for years. We were friends long before we became lovers, and there was something different between us than with any other guy I'd known. He'd always been there to pick me up when I was down.

"So what did you want to talk to me about? You said in your text you had something to tell me."

Now that we were breaking up, there was no sense to tell him about my arrangement with Paxton. It was probably best he didn't know. "It's nothing really," I answered, stepping back. "My brother called and told me to take a few weeks off. I was just a little excited about it."

Bradley gazed down at me and brushed a strand of my hair away from my cheek. "So the time I have to leave California is the time you have off. Talk about irony."

He was leaving? "Where are you going?"

His whole demeanor changed and his lips curved into a small smile. "I wanted to tell you this before, but you've been kind of busy. I'm headed to New York. Apparently, they're interested in me."

"Bradley, that's amazing," I squealed. "Will you be playing with Colin?"

Reaching for his hat, he nodded and put it on. "You're damn right. We're gonna tear it up in the major leagues. I just don't know how I'm going to get used to New York. It's not exactly the place I thought I'd call home."

"You'll get used to it," I told him lamely, knowing I couldn't give him the comfort he needed. It wasn't my job anymore.

We stared at each other for I don't know how long. All of our shared memories flooded my mind and made my chest ache. Tears came to my eyes, not from sorrow, but the heaviness of it all. This was a chapter of my life coming to an end.

Opening the door, he stepped out but I wasn't ready to let him go just yet, so I walked out with him. Side by side, we strolled down the stairs, my throat constricting tighter with each step. "You'll do fine," I assured him, choking out the words. "I'm so proud of you and how much you've accomplished."

By the time we got down to his truck it took all I had not to let my tears fall. He unlocked his door and was about to open it before he scooped me up into his arms and squeezed. "Goddammit, I didn't realize how hard this was going to be. As much as I've spent the last couple of months pissed off, I'm going to miss the hell out of you."

I chuckled as my tears finally fell. "Same here. Especially our fights. You sure knew how to push my buttons."

"It's just part of my charm, babe. Maybe I'll give you a call sometime and we can fight."

After he let me go, I lifted up on my tiptoes and placed a chaste kiss on his lips and brushed my hands through his hair. It was the last time we'd ever share an embrace. "I look forward to it. Just don't forget me when you're all big and bad in New York."

"What about you? I bet next season you'll have a title. You'll be the one forgetting me."

"That's never going to happen," I said, taking a step back.

Opening his truck door, he got in and smiled down at me. "I'll talk to you soon, Gabby. Don't get into any trouble."

With a sly smile, I winked up at him. "Can't promise you that. Be careful in New York."

Even though I was smiling and I was glad it ended on good terms, I could feel the hole in my heart growing. His truck roared to life and he glanced down at me, mouthing the word 'goodbye' before driving out of the parking lot. As soon as his truck disappeared, I turned on my heel and headed for the stairs in a fog, keeping my gaze on the ground as I walked.

Eyes blurry, I ran smack dab into a wall and almost fell over, but a set of hands grabbed onto my arms, keeping me in place. Once stable, the guy let me go and I quickly rubbed my eyes and looked up at him. It definitely wasn't a wall I ran into. On the contrary, it was a tall, young man—a few years older than me—with ash blond hair and chocolate brown eyes. He was shirtless and sweaty, with blue running shorts hanging low on his hips.

"I am so sorry," I apologized. "I should've watched where I was going."

"No problem. I'm glad I could help. My name's Cliff," he replied, holding out his hand. "I just moved in upstairs a couple of days ago."

Taking his warm hand, I shook it and let go. "It's nice to meet you. I'm Gabriella. I live upstairs too." I started up the steps and he followed alongside me.

"Not that it's any of my business, but are you okay?" he asked. "You look upset."

"It's never easy when you end a relationship."

We were already to the second floor and he kept going to the third. He must be my neighbor. "Trust me, I know how that goes. I just got back from a tour in Iraq and came home to find my fiancé fucking another man—in our bed."

"Ouch," I muttered. That had to suck ass. My situation was nowhere near as bad as his. "So you're in the military?" My eyes couldn't help but roam over his perfectly toned muscles. He was definitely built to be a fighter.

"I was," he answered, grinning over at me. "I decided not to reenlist. Once I got home and realized everyone's lives had moved on while I was away, I decided to pack my shit up and move. I like it better here anyway."

We finally got to my door and I stopped. "Well, this is me," I said.

"And that's me," he countered, pointing to the door diagonal to mine. "I'm surprised you didn't hear me moving in this week."

"I wasn't here. I was visiting my friends at their cabin."

"Ah, I see. Well, Gabriella, it was nice meeting you. I'm sure I'll see you around." He turned to walk off, looking over his shoulder and smiling before opening the door to his apartment.

I had a freaking hottie for a neighbor. Too bad he did nothing for me. My traitorous body wanted what I didn't want it to have. And I definitely wasn't going to give in.

CHAPTER 2

Gabriella

IT WAS ALREADY Sunday, and I had no clue what time he would be at my place. I resolved myself to face the facts . . . I needed to get ready. What would've been a twenty minute packing job took me almost three hours. I wanted to kick myself in the ass when I questioned every single thing I put in my suitcase. I shouldn't care what I looked like in front of Paxton, but I did. I hated myself for it.

My phone buzzed and I couldn't help feel it was fate texting.

Paxton: Be there in ten.
Me: Yippee…
Me: Why can't I just drive to your house?

Paxton: This way I know you can't run.

The more I convinced myself I didn't want to go, the more I'd believe it. If I kept pounding that idea in my head, I would eventually have to think it was true, right?

Opening the refrigerator, I opened a bottle of wine and chugged it. I only got in a few gulps before Paxton knocked on the door. I strolled over to the door and opened it wide, bringing the bottle to my lips. His eyes went wide and he let out a deep belly laugh. I didn't see what was so funny.

"I'm turning into an alcoholic over this shit. You might want to rethink your terms," I grumbled.

Coming inside, Paxton took the bottle from my hands and placed it on the counter. He was dressed in a pair of khaki shorts and a neon green T-shirt that looked amazingly hot on his tanned skin. *Fuck, I need more wine.*

"Not going to happen, sunshine. If you resort to binge drinking I know just how to sober you up. Or better yet, drink more and maybe it'll loosen you up. I'm sure we could have a little bit of fun. Your boyfriend would hate it though." By the smirk and the lustful look in his eyes, I knew what he had in mind. No more alcohol for me . . . unfortunately. "I trust you handled that situation already?"

Gritting my teeth, I rolled my eyes and nodded. "You have nothing to worry about. He's gone."

"For good?" he asked, wide-eyed.

"Can we not talk about it?" I snapped. Out of the corner of my eye I saw the smug bastard smile.

"Sure thing, sunshine. I would be more than happy to not talk about your douchebag ex, it leaves room to do *other* things. In fact, I think I know what'll help. Is that what you're bringing to my house?" he asked, nodding toward my three suitcases sitting on the floor.

I waltzed over and lifted the handle to one of them. "Yes, this is it. And how exactly do you think you're going to help?"

"You'll see."

"The only way you could make me happy is to let me stay home. Trust me, you'll probably hate me once this month is over."

Before I could get out the door, he blocked it with his arm and leaned over, his warm breath fanning across my neck. "Fighting this will only make it worse, Gabby. You can lie all you want, but I can always tell when you're not giving me the truth."

"That's ridiculous," I scoffed, tucking my hair behind my ear. "I'm not lying."

"Then you should get rid of that nervous tick of yours."

"What the fuck are you talking about?" I brought my hand up to my ear and tucked my hair behind it . . . . Quickly, I dropped my hand to my side and cleared my throat. Standing up straighter, I held my head high. "Can we go already?"

His deep chuckle made me shiver. "Sure thing, doll." He bopped me on the bottom of my chin with his finger. "You might want to put on tennis shoes though."

Furrowing my brows, I looked down at my sandals. "Why?" My tennis shoes were in my suitcase, so I opened it up and switched them out.

"Because we're going to go out and have some fun. You look like you could use it." He winked and nudged me out the door. After I had it locked, I followed him down the stairs to his Hummer.

"I hope you know this isn't a date," I stated adamantly.

Opening the back door, he slid my suitcases in and chuckled. "Get in."

After he shut his door, we were on our way. I had no clue where we were going, or where he even lived. There was no turning back, only going forward. To be honest, it scared the shit out of me.

Ever since Paxton and I had kissed a couple of weeks ago, things had been awkward and tense between us. It wasn't so bad when we were around other people, but as soon as we were alone, my mind would wander. The day it happened I was training late at Carter's gym. It just so happened it was a night Paxton stayed past closing too. He wasn't comfortable with me being there by myself, and to be honest, I wanted him there. I was up in the ring, pounding one of the dummy punching bags when he decided to glove up and help me.

When he took me down to the mat, I had been at his mercy, bound with his hands holding my wrists and his body close between my legs. The closer he moved, the harder my heart pounded in my chest. I let him kiss me and probably would've gone further if my phone hadn't interrupted us. I took it as a sign that I'd be making a horrible mistake if I let him fuck me. Not only would it have pissed my brother off, but just the thought of sleeping with the enemy weighed me down with guilt.

"What are you thinking about over there?" Paxton asked.

We had been in the car for about an hour and I refused to look at him. My traitorous body reacted to him like a dog in heat. What the fuck was wrong with me? I wanted to fight him, yet I yearned to submit to him.

His voice broke through my inner monologue. "Are you not going to talk to me?"

This time, I turned my attention to him. "I'm sorry, I was just thinking. Where exactly are we going? I didn't realize you lived so far out."

His smile made me shiver. "I don't, but I told you there was somewhere I wanted to take you. We're almost there, and then afterward we'll go to my place. I have a house in Manhattan Beach."

"Must be nice," I mumbled to myself.

I didn't have the money like my brother and all of his friends did. He'd even paid for my schooling, which I'd always be forever grateful for. And now that my mother owned her own salon, she had a decent wage coming in.

I'd won a few fights now, which brought in a decent amount of cash, but in order to get more, I had to fight. Being in the UFC, you never knew exactly when your fights would be. It was always last minute, which meant I needed to be ready. Taking the next six weeks off wouldn't be doable if I had a fight, but I really felt like my body needed it.

"I have a question," I started. Paxton looked at me and lifted his brows. "Did you make more money fighting in the UFC, or when you were fighting illegally?"

Sighing, he turned his attention back to the road. "Illegally. There were nights I'd bring in a hundred grand or more. Don't get me wrong, it was fucking awesome, but I wouldn't go back to it. It was a dark time in my past."

"What made you decide to get out?"

His jaw clenched and his knuckles turned white on the steering wheel. "It's not something I like to talk about."

I'd seen the brutality of the fights in the underground world. I watched a man get his arm sliced off by a sword for Christ's sake. It was almost like watching a horror movie, yet real. If Paxton had to do shit like that it made me wonder what kind of man he was on the inside. He didn't get the nickname Reaper for no reason. The thought made me shiver.

"Are you cold?" He glanced down at my arms and trailed a finger up my bare skin making my skin break out in chills.

Moving my arm, I rubbed the skin he touched, willing the bumps away. "No, I'm fine. I was just thinking about the nickname they gave you. I can only imagine what you had to do to earn that."

He pulled us into a parking lot and parked, turning his concerned gaze my way. "Does that scare you? Not knowing what I've done?"

Did it scare me? *Hell yeah.* "Kind of," I admitted truthfully. "Our actions make us who we are. You were friends with Kyle, so obviously you had to be okay with the bad shit he did to people, including my brother."

Jaw firm, he took a deep breath, his stare never wavering. "You know, I'm glad we're talking about this because now you have no choice but to listen. I was only friends with Kyle for Kacey's sake. And speaking of which, I'd like to know how you see her? She's Kyle's sister which obviously makes her bad too, right?"

Actually, she wasn't bad at all. I liked her. Paxton waited on my comeback but I didn't have one. "Okay, you have a point," I gave in. "We aren't always like the friends we hang out with. But even if you weren't one of Kyle's friends, it still doesn't change who you are. You're just like the rest of the fighters. Any piece of ass that comes your way, you're gonna want it. I've been around you guys for a long time now."

Paxton snorted and opened his door. "Well, I guess your brother is a real dick to his wife then. Why don't you stop now, you're not making any valid points."

Pursing my lips, I watched him get out of the car with a smug smile on his face. He got me and he knew it. What a pain in the ass. When I got out of the car, I slammed the door and looked around. I had no clue where we were. There were shopping centers all around, but he parked us at a huge warehouse off to the side. I'd never been in this area before.

"What is this place?" I asked.

His smile widened. "Come and find out."

Starting toward the warehouse, I walked beside him through the parking lot until we got to the door. When I looked inside, my eyes widened. "Oh my God, you can't be serious." Inside was a race track, with professional go karts. Ones that actually had speed. I hadn't been on one in years.

"Are you ready to race? I have to say I'm kind of good."

Little did he know I had experience with racing machines. When my brother started earning money in the ring, he moved us all to a better house and surprised me with my very own go kart. We could never afford to do things when we were younger, so he made sure to bring back my childhood. He even had a race track made in our backyard so I could race against the boys in school. It was so much fun.

Paxton opened the door and I grinned from ear to ear. "Better watch out. I'm pretty good myself."

"Really?" he replied. "How about we make a wager on it if you think you're so good?"

"Okay, how about if I win, you lower the terms from one month to two weeks?" I held out my hand and dared him to take the challenge. There was no way he could beat me. I had this shit on lock.

"Agreed," he said, shaking my hand. "Let's see what you got."

CHAPTER 3

Paxton

GABRIELLA THOUGHT SHE could fool me, but I knew she had experience in racing. In fact, she'd be absolutely stunned to know who I had in my back pocket. There were more people rooting for us to get together than just me.

After putting on our jumpsuits and helmets, the guys at the track gave me and Gabriella full access to the track so we could race by ourselves. Side by side, we sat in our karts, revving our engines at the start line. I was focused and kept my attention on the red lights. As soon as the green lights lit, we were both off, squealing our tires.

I was good at racing, but not so much with little go karts. No one really knew what I did in my spare time. I hoped to show Gabby soon, as I had a race coming up and I wanted her to be there. Even if I had to cut our time down to two weeks, it was still more than enough to wear her down. She needed to know there was more to me than just fighting.

Turn after turn, we kept up with each other's pace, neither one of us taking the lead. She rammed into me a few times, but I corrected myself and kept up with her. I honestly thought I was going to have to slow it down for her, but she was doing better than anyone I'd ever seen, including myself. Her lines were perfect and she sailed through the track like it was nothing. I had to say I was impressed.

Two laps down and one more to go. Tension ran high, but I could see the light in her eyes when she peered over at me. We had two more turns and then it was the straight away to the finish line. With my foot all the way down on the gas, I floored it forward, but Gabriella never left my side. Once the line was crossed, we both slammed on the brakes and came to a screeching stop.

Gabriella unstrapped her helmet and laughed. "I *so* beat you, Pax."

Getting out of the kart, I lifted up my helmet and shook my head. "Sorry, sunshine, but you're wrong. Let's see what the guys have to say."

All three workers were standing by the monitor looking at the video. By the looks on their faces, I'd say they didn't know who won. It was too close to call.

"What's the verdict, guys?" Gabriella asked them.

They were young, probably in their early twenties and they didn't know what to say. Even when Gabriella looked at the screen, her brows furrowed. "Hmm . . . it kind of looks like a tie."

"That's what I said," one of the guys said. "I guess

it's up to you two."

All three of them walked off and left us at the screen. It really did look like it was a tie. "You surprised me. I didn't think you had it in you," I teased.

Holding her helmet in her hand, she smiled up at me. It was the first time I'd seen a genuine smile on her face since she'd been with me. "What can I say? I'm a natural."

"So what do you want to do about the terms? If you want to take the two weeks off of the month, you can. You totally kicked ass out there."

We started toward the prep room to return our gear, but she stopped me with a hand on my arm. "You would do that even if I didn't clearly win?"

Smirking, I opened the door to the prep room and placed my helmet back on the shelf and my jumpsuit in the basket. "You earned the two weeks off. To be fair, however, you should know that if you cut out those weeks, you'll be making it up by doubling the amount of time we spend together. It's your choice though."

She groaned and took off her jumpsuit. "I swear I knew there had to be a reason you agreed to the bet. Fine, I'll take the two weeks. I might as well get them over with instead of prolonging it."

"Are you sure that's what you want?" I asked, holding open the front door.

With her head held high, she threw her jumpsuit in the basket and sauntered past me. "Yep. I'm positive the more time you spend with me, the more you're going to want me to leave."

Well, *that* wasn't going to happen.

CHAPTER 4

Gabriella

I THOUGHT FOR sure I would win the race, but Paxton was pretty damn good. The whole way to his house he kept a smug smile on his face as if he knew something I didn't. Did I make a mistake compacting our month into two weeks? I was starting to think I did.

"When we get to my house, feel free to look anywhere you want. It's yours for the next two weeks."

"Does that mean I can sleep in any room I want?" I asked.

"If that's what you want."

"And you're not going to come sneaking in there after dark? How do I know I can trust you?"

He pressed a button below the overhead lights that opened the gate in front of his house. "How do I know I can trust *you*?" he countered. "You might try to sneak into my room for all I know."

Snorting, I rolled my eyes. "I'm not desperate."

As he drove us down his driveway, he kept a grin on his face. He didn't believe a word I said, and it aggravated the crap out of me. Although, the thought of secretly going into his room *was* kind of tempting. I could imagine walking in there, his bare skin illuminated with a faint glow of the moon.

There were many nights I'd had forbidden dreams of him touching me, even when I was lying in bed with Bradley. Just thinking about pressing my body against his made my insides clench and throb. It was completely fucked up the way my body wanted him. I always thought it was men who wanted things they couldn't have, but I was wrong.

Once we got closer to his house, I gazed up in amazement. It was a two story mansion made out of beautiful stones that gave it an earthy feel to it. Paxton didn't take me for the type of guy to live in a house like that.

"Your house is gorgeous," I admired.

Getting out of the car, I walked over to the walkway beside the house and peered out at the waves rolling in. *Hell yeah, we're right on the beach.* The smell of the salty sea air and the water crashing in reminded me of my other passion, marine biology. There was going to come a time when I'd no longer be able to fight, and when that time came, I was going to put my degree to use.

Paxton came up to me and bumped me in the arm. "Why don't you come pick out a room and then we'll eat our dinner on the beach?"

"Yes," I blurted a little too eagerly. "That'd be great." *Way to sound desperate, Gabby.* I might as well have laid down and asked him to fuck me right here in the driveway.

Following him inside, he set my bags down on the floor and I immediately sighed when the smell of rosemary and onions overtook my senses. "Gabriella, there's someone I'd like you to meet."

I was meeting someone? We followed the delicious scent down a hallway, until we got to the kitchen. There was a short lady by the stove with curly, brown hair and glasses. She had to be in her early to mid-fifties. When she saw me come in, she smiled and waved. Paxton stood by her side and reached into one of the pots on the stove, pulling out a roasted carrot and popping it into his mouth.

"Gabriella, this is my Aunt Jackie. She also happens to be a personal chef. I've been lucky enough to have her for a while, but now she's moving on to bigger and better clients." He grabbed another carrot and she swatted him with her spatula.

Jackie laughed and looked over at me. "Don't listen to him, sweetheart. He's actually a decent cook, but if he listened to me he'd be amazing. Sadly, he's a little stubborn."

"I can't argue with you there," I quipped. "I've told him to leave me alone plenty of times and he still hasn't taken the hint."

"That's my nephew for you," she giggled, taking off her apron and hanging it on the wall inside the large pantry. "All right, son, the chicken and homemade bread is in the oven. Everything else is up here on the stove." Opening the pots, Paxton glanced in them and smiled. "If you need anything don't hesitate to call."

"I'm sure I can manage," he said with a wink.

"Gabriella, it was nice meeting you. From what I

hear, it looks like I'll be seeing more of you." This time she was the one who winked at Paxton.

I smiled at her as she walked past and glared at Paxton when I heard the front door shut. "Did you tell her I'm going to be here for the next few weeks?" I asked incredulously.

Paxton chuckled and pulled out the chicken and loaf of bread out of the oven. "Yep, which is the other reason why she's not going to be cooking for me anymore."

"Oh, so you expect me to do it? Is that one of my duties while I'm here?" I grumbled. I could cook, but I wasn't an expert chef like his aunt.

"I figured we could figure it out together."

"Does that mean you'll be wearing an apron?" I asked, holding back my giggle. I watched him move around the kitchen and the first thing that came to mind was seeing him in the apron with nothing else underneath it. It was a delicious, forbidden fantasy.

Paxton smirked and turned his heated stare to mine. "Let me just tell you how all of this is going to work." Now he had my undivided attention. "If you want something from me, I have to get something in return. It's a give and give thing here. I'm not going to demand anything you don't want to give. But if you want something of me, it's going to cost you. Keep that in mind, sunshine."

"Duly noted. I won't demand a thing."

He chuckled. "We'll see about that."

I had restraint and I sure as hell was going to utilize it. As long as he kept his distance I'd be okay. It was only for two weeks.

Once our dinner was put together and loaded up in a basket, we made our way down to the beach. There was hardly anyone around, which was fine by me. I hated crowded beaches. As we walked, I cringed every time I saw a plastic bottle or trash littering the ground. When I was in high school, I'd been in the Environmental Club and I took that shit seriously. I guess that was why I wanted to major in a science field in college.

Since I had the blanket, I draped it on the sand so Pax could set the basket down. The sunset was just off in the distance, casting the sky in a pink and yellow haze. It was the perfect setting for a date. It was a shame I wasn't on one.

"So, your aunt?" I began. "Is she on your mother's side or your father's?"

"Mother's," he answered. "She got custody of me after my parents died."

I started to help him with the food and paused. "Oh no, I'm so sorry. I didn't mean to bring it up."

He smiled sadly and passed me a plate. "No need to be sorry. It was a long time ago. I was in high school when it happened."

"Do you want to talk about it?"

Keeping his eyes on the food, he pulled out the chicken and potatoes while I grabbed my favorite thing . . . the homemade bread. "My parents loved to go sailing. Sometimes they would take me with them when I was little.

25

When I got into high school and started dating Kacey I stopped going with them. I had my own life, you know?"

"Oh, I get it. Alas, I didn't have loving parents like that. I mean my mother was great, but she was all I had along with Matt. My father left when I was three." Setting his plate on the blanket, he laid down and rested on his elbow, facing me but keeping his eyes on the ocean while he ate. "How did they die?" I asked.

He popped a piece of bread in his mouth and chewed it slowly. "There was a big storm that came through off the coast of Fiji. They were trying to get to land before it hit, but they didn't make it in time. I guess you can say I spent a lot of my high school years angry. I didn't start getting into trouble until after that. Kacey kind of kept me grounded."

It was strange to think that Kacey, the girl who stole Tyler's heart, had also stolen Paxton's once before. I should be jealous, but I wasn't. She helped get Tyler to where he needed to be. He couldn't get that with me.

"So Kacey helped you?"

He smiled and finally looked at me. "She was everything to me. At least, until we moved on. Is that how Bradley was with you? Are you upset that you two aren't together anymore?"

I took my time chewing my bread and turned my head. Bradley was my friend and lover, but he wasn't *everything* to me. I'd never had that. "No, it wasn't like that with us," I murmured. "Don't get me wrong, I feel the loss of him here," I said, rubbing a hand over my heart. "But I'm honestly not that upset about it. Our time had come to an end."

"So you don't blame me?"

I shook my head. "No."

"Why can't you look at me and say that?"

Turning to him, I looked him straight in the eyes. "No, I don't blame you, Paxton. I don't think I've really been in love with anyone before. I loved Tyler and Bradley, but with Bradley it was more of a friend kind of love and with Tyler it was pretty much all lust."

Then it hit me. That sharp feeling in my chest wasn't hurt or sadness, it was envy, longing. I wanted to feel that kind of love. All of my friends were gone, scattered. Having Ashleigh around helped me to not feel so lonely. Now she was gone.

"What's that look for? You seem upset," Paxton remarked, grabbing my attention.

"Sorry, I was just thinking. I didn't really realize what my problem was until just now."

"What are you talking about?"

Swallowing hard, I fiddled around with my food so I wouldn't have to look at him. The words were on the tip of my tongue, but if I said them out loud I wouldn't be able to take them back. It would show my vulnerability and I didn't want that. The only problem was, I didn't have anyone else to talk to. How in the hell did it get to the point where Paxton Emerson was literally all I had?

"I just realized I'm alone now," I whispered. "All of my friends are gone." If I was honest with myself, I should be thanking him for making me stay with him. At least now I wasn't physically alone.

His hand came down on mine, soft yet strong. "No, you're not, Gabby. Because I'm here, and as long as you're with me, you'll never be alone. I promise."

CHAPTER 5

Gabriella

AFTER OUR DINNER on the beach, I had felt embarrassed admitting my insecurities so once we got back, I retreated to the first bedroom I could find and closed myself up. Paxton was actually being nice, but I shut myself off and ran away.

When morning arrived, I quietly got out of bed and threw on a pair of shorts and a tank top. Surely, he had a gym in his monstrosity of a house. Or better yet, some breakfast.

Sneaking out of the room, I tiptoed downstairs and into the kitchen. My stomach growled and I was thirsty as hell. He had a Keurig machine and it reminded me of how I wanted my pumpkin spice coffee. Maybe I could steal one of his many cars and go get some. Instead, I opted for a glass of orange juice and a bowl of corn flakes. It was interesting searching through his cabinets. There were the occasional bags of potato chips, but he also had some fruits and vegetables too. His aunt must've done his shopping.

What I wasn't expecting while eating my cereal was what I found in the freezer. A corn flake went down the wrong way and I choked, hacking as if I was dying.

"Gabby, what the fuck, are you okay?" Paxton shouted as he rushed into the kitchen.

My throat was burning, but I was fine. "Yeah, I'm okay. My cereal just went down the wrong way. I was just a little shocked when I opened the freezer." That was when I got a good look at him. He was wearing a white tank top and jeans, all covered in grease. If I thought I couldn't breathe before, I definitely couldn't now. "Holy shitfuck." Wait, did I just say that out loud?

"I think my aunt went a little overboard," he said, rubbing the back of his neck. The tank top showed off both of his arms which were covered from shoulder to wrist in tattoos. On his tanned skin, it was sexy as hell.

Closing my gaping mouth, I cleared my throat and pointed to the freezer. "You think? I bet there's two hundred dollars worth of Ben & Jerry's in there."

Chuckling, he walked over to the freezer and opened it up. "That doesn't surprise me. Jackie didn't know what flavor to get, so she got them all, and then some. All I told her was that you liked it."

"And how did you know that?"

He snorted and shut the freezer door. "Every time you and Ashleigh were around each other you couldn't get through a conversation without talking about it. Besides,

Ryley told me Ashleigh was the same way."

"Probably even more so now that she's pregnant," I said, laughing. "Anyway, thank you. It'll make the stay definitely more enjoyable."

"Well, fuck, I was hoping *I* would make it more enjoyable."

The smile on his face was contagious and I couldn't help but return it even though I knew I shouldn't. "How long have you been up?" I asked, taking a seat at the bar. I still needed to finish my cereal. Honestly, I didn't think he'd be awake. It was still fairly early.

"A while. I've been out in my garage."

"I can tell," I replied, gazing up and down his body. "Doing what?"

"Why don't you come and see? Do you need to meet your brother at the gym today?"

I shook my head. "No, he's taking a few weeks off. I don't have to go there."

A wide grin spread across his face. "Well, now that we're both taking off some time, we can actually enjoy life outside of a gym."

I scoffed. "That's what you think. Matt will kill me if I don't work out during this time off. Surely, you have a gym in here somewhere."

He narrowed his gaze skeptically. "You haven't been looking around the house while I've been outside?"

I had a mouthful of cereal but I didn't care. "I made it as far as the freezer. I mean really, I'm not going to go searching through your house. Furthermore, I thought you were still in bed. The last thing I wanted to do was walk in on you."

"Yeah," he agreed, smirking. "You wouldn't want to

accidentally see me in an indecent situation."

Now I was thinking about him touching himself. *Fucking great*.

Turning on his heel, he headed for the door and called out over his shoulder. "If you want to know where the gym is, it's above my garage. I'll meet you out there."

After the door shut, I hurried with my cereal and rushed upstairs to brush my teeth and wash my face. I really wanted to find his room, but knowing my luck, he'd walk in and find me. That was the last thing I needed. Once I put my tennis shoes on, I was ready to go. Paxton had two garages, one connected to his house, while the other was off to the side. It was much larger and had a second floor. From the music blaring, it had to be in that one.

The door was open, so I made my way in and walked past the covered cars toward the stairs. It smelled like oil and lubrication sprays. There were black stains all over the floor where Paxton must have been working. I had no idea he could work on vehicles. Sometimes it was hard to picture fighters doing anything other than fighting. Our schedules were always so demanding and there wasn't ever time to do much of anything other than eat, sleep, train, and fight.

Heading up the stairs, I could see Paxton through the crack in the door, lifting his weights. He's changed into a pair of shorts and his skin was shiny with sweat. Was it bad I wanted to lick him? *What the hell. Get your shit together, woman.* No, I didn't want to lick him or do anything else that involved touching his body with mine. Fighters were off limits, especially him.

Standing up straight, I opened the door and waltzed in, getting the full view of the room. He had everything you could ever need to train, with one exception—a practice ring. He did, however, have a large mat that could suffice. I sat down on the mat and began to stretch, feeling the pull as the muscles lengthened.

"Have you told anyone you are here?" he asked, coming to the mat.

He joined me on the floor and started stretching too. "Ashleigh. I called and told her the day you came over. I haven't talked to her since then though."

"What about your brother?"

"Oh God, no. He'd kill me if he knew I was here. He refuses to let me get involved with you guys. Why do you think Tyler and I kept our affair a secret?"

"Yeah, but if nothing's going on, what do you have to hide?"

"Seriously?" I said, glaring at him. "The last thing you need is for me to have to explain the real reason why I'm here. We'd both get in trouble if anyone found out."

"So basically you're saying you'd care if Scar came after me? I'm a little shocked, considering how you loathe me."

Getting to my feet, he did the same and stared down at me, waiting. "I don't hate you, Paxton. I just don't care for you. I appreciate what you did for Ryley and Ashleigh and I'm paying my debt. That's all this is."

He stepped closer. "Is it? Because I don't think you know what you want. Or maybe you do and you're just too afraid to admit it."

When I moved back, he countered. "You're wrong," I whispered, feeling the chills fan across my skin. He was about to attack and I knew it, I could feel it. Practicing with my brother and Ryley was one thing, but with Paxton it was a whole different story.

"What are you doing?" I demanded.

With a wolfish grin, he circled around me like a lion hunting its prey. "You said your brother wanted you to train, right? Well, I'm going to help you. We all fight differently and I think you could benefit from my style."

"I'm quite happy with my own," I said, slowly getting into stance. My body tingled in anticipation.

"Yeah, but if my moves could help you win the title, it's a win-win."

My chest rose and fell as my body went on hyper alert. Paxton was good at his floor game and if he took me down to the mat I didn't know if I'd have the strength to fight him. Deep down I've wanted to get back in the ring with him. Now I had my wish. Instead of waiting, I swung and he blocked me, smiling as he deflected each and every jab. Paxton was the Light Heavyweight champion and outweighed me by about fifty pounds. There was no way I could fight someone like him and actually win.

The muscles in his thighs twitched and I knew he was about to charge. Luckily, I jumped out of the way in time. I'd watched him train plenty of times, studying his moves. That was what a good fighter did, they studied their opponents and other fighters. Matt taught me to always be vigilant.

"Very good," he remarked.

"What can I say, I'm quick on my feet." He deflected every single swing and kick which started to piss me off. It made me realize how inexperienced I was compared to him. But I had my ways. They might be dirty, but I could definitely put them to good use.

Straightening my stance, I sauntered over to him,

smiling lazily. He lifted his brows and placed his hands on his hips, never once taking his eyes off of me. "What are you doing?"

My smile grew wider and once I got close enough, I swiped my leg behind his and used the force of my body to make him fall back. We both fell to the mat and I landed on top of him. Before I could shout out my triumph, he quickly wrapped his arms around my waist and tumbled me over. Now his body was on top of mine.

"Dammit," I hissed as my head slammed down on the mat. "I thought I had you."

His face was close to mine, lips almost touching. The weight of his body pressed into mine, his hips digging into my own. However, it wasn't just his hips pressing into me. My body welcomed his touch and grew wet just having him against me. I also couldn't move because in our grapple he had taken my wrists and held my arms above my head, pinning me to the floor.

"And you almost did, sunshine. But now I have you at *my* mercy."

I tried to move, but he held on tighter, smiling smugly down at me. "You can let me up any day now."

"No, I kind of like where I'm at." His smile faded, and then turned serious. "As much as I like having you where you are, there's something you need to learn."

"What?" I whispered.

The grip he had on my wrists tightened. "Never, under any circumstances, let another man immobilize your arms like this."

"I fight women, Pax. I don't think I'll ever be in the ring fighting a man."

"That's not what I'm talking about. For right now, the

only person who's going to be holding you down like this is me. Nevertheless, sometimes it doesn't always work like that."

The haunted look in his eyes made me shiver. He had to be thinking about Kacey and what almost happened to her. The night she was held against her will and was almost raped, while he was in the ring fighting for his title. He wanted to go after her, but Tyler needed him to stay so everything would look normal. I'd never seen him look at another girl the way he looked at Kacey that night.

"Do you still love her?" I asked.

Paxton loosened his grip and let my wrists go, but still kept his weight on me. "Not in the way you think. It's hard not to think about that night. I just get so angry. That's why I want you to be prepared if anything like this ever happened to you."

"I know how to defend myself."

"You're right, but there's no way in hell you can defend yourself against someone like me. That's why I'm going to show you what to do. Most guys are going to take you to the floor and you'll be in this position. You can punch the shit out of them all you want, but all it's going to do is piss them off. Knowing you, that's exactly what you'd do."

I looked up at him. "What am I supposed to do then, lay there?"

"Yes. And most importantly you need to concentrate. When someone takes you down you have a split second to react. Do you see this?" he asked, putting his hands on the floor by both sides of my head. When I nodded, he continued. "Okay, with my arms like this, you need to bring yours up between mine and sweep them out from under me. That'll make me lose my balance and fall forward.

"Before I do that, you take the palm of your hand and jab it upwards toward my nose. That type of blow will make the nose break, eyes water, and your attacker to lose focus. Afterward, you can always beat the shit out of him and run away."

Grabbing my wrists, he pulled me up to my feet. "Now let's practice it. Just don't break my nose."

I winked and got into position. "I'll try not to."

As soon as I was ready, he went on the attack and took me back down to the mat. Before he could grab my wrists, I did what he said and swiped his own arms out from under him and stopped with my palm at his nose. When I moved my hand aside, he smirked down at me.

"That's fucking amazing. I honestly didn't think you'd get it that fast."

"I'm a quick learner," I murmured breathlessly. "Thanks for showing me."

"You're welcome."

He laid there, star-fished on top of me. I could feel his heartbeat thumping and see the sweat above his brow. I instinctively clenched my lower stomach and his dick lengthened between us. I waited for him to move his lips toward mine, but he stayed in place, staring me down.

Ever so slowly, he moved his lips closer to mine and I parted my own slightly, closing my eyes. "Well," he said, startling my eyes back open, "I think that's enough for today." Hopping off me, he put out his hand to help me get up.

What a whirlwind. I'd thought for sure he was going to kiss me. I was going to need to change my underwear. "Do you mind if I run by my apartment? I forgot some things." It was the only thing I could think of to say.

"Sure, take the Hummer. I'll just be here."

He started lifting his weights while I stood there watching him, feeling completely out of sorts. I was just so used to him chasing me, always trying to get in my pants. I guess I stood there a little too long because he had stopped lifting and was looking at me cockeyed.

"The keys are on the kitchen counter. Was there something else?"

I stood there hoping he would talk a little more, but he kept going as if I wasn't there. I wasn't sure I like this change of behavior. *How odd.*

By the time I got to my apartment and trudged up the steps, I felt like a complete fool. I had laid under Paxton and closed my eyes, opening myself up to him, and he had done nothing. Was I the only one who felt something? Maybe he was done with my refusals. How much could one man take before his dignity was bruised?

Pulling out my keys, I had them ready to unlock my door when something caught my eye. Lying across the rug at the front door laid a single, black rose with a red ribbon tied around the stem. A note was attached, but I couldn't open it unless I untied the ribbon. Who the hell would leave me a black rose? Surely, it wasn't Bradley?

Once my door was unlocked, I walked inside and shut it. I untied the red silk slowly, so as to not prick my fingers on the thorns. There was no name on the outside of the paper, but when I finally had it free, I opened it up. Furrowing my brows, I read the words:

Flipping it over, there was nothing on the back. What the hell did that mean? All I knew was, it didn't settle well with me. My spine prickled and my hair stood on end. The only reason I wanted to come home was to grab my pumpkin spice coffee. That was exactly what I did. I grabbed the box and put it under my arm, staring at the rose. I didn't like the flower; there was something ominous about it. Leaving it on the counter, I snatched up Paxton's keys and walked out the door, making sure to lock it behind me. I was ready to get back.

CHAPTER 6

Paxton

I WANTED GABRIELLA so bad I couldn't fucking see straight. My balls ached like a bitch and what was worse, I knew she wanted me too. I just needed her to make the first move. But she was too goddamned stubborn to do anything about it. The second I heard her leave the driveway, I picked up my phone and dialed the number I needed.

"Hey, Pax," she answered. "How's it going?"

"Not fast enough. Miss Stubborn refuses to face the fact she wants me."

"You could stop waiting for her to come to you, and just tell her the truth," she suggested. "Seriously, I know she wants to be with you. The only thing keeping her back is feeling like a traitor to her brother. He's the one who doesn't want her with any of you. The truth will set you free," she laughed.

"That's not the point, Ashleigh. Yeah, I could tell her the truth, but I don't want to list reasons why she should be with me. I need her to admit she wants me, against all odds."

"Good luck with that, Paxton. She's strong like bull. But, I think you're right. She likes a challenge and hates to be forced into a corner."

"Don't worry, I know just what to do. I don't need luck." *I need a fucking miracle.*

I was sitting by the pool when Gabriella finally got back. As soon as she sat beside me, I got up and stretched, making her eyes go wide.

"Where are you going? I just got here," she remarked.

"Yeah, sorry about that . . . I have plans for the evening. I'll see you in the morning though, okay?"

"In the morning?"

Stopping by the patio door, I looked back at her. She looked stunned. "I'm probably not making it home tonight, sunshine. There are hash browns and eggs in the fridge, and of course, you've got the keys to my Hummer. Have a good one, call me if you need anything."

Turning on my heel, I went straight to my room and didn't look back. This plan had to work. She might not give in tonight or tomorrow, but by the end of the week if this didn't work, I didn't know what would.

CHAPTER 7

Gabriella

FOR THREE DAYS, Paxton and I had worked out together, but then he always had other things to do, leaving me to my own devices. When I tried to talk to him he was pleasant, but that was it. No flirting. No *extra* attention. Was he over me? I started to doubt that he really even wanted to finish out the rest of the two weeks. I had thought about just leaving and not coming back, but in all honesty, I didn't want to go back to my empty apartment.

I guess I could always visit Ashleigh and Ryley in the mountains, but I wouldn't because I was pissed off. It took me awhile to come to terms with it all, but I was thoroughly upset Pax didn't want me. I needed to verify his feelings, and soon.

Putting on the skimpiest bathing suit I had, I strolled

through the house and out to the pool. Every day after working on the cars, he always walked through the patio door once he was done. He had an old Model T and a vintage Chevy Corvette he was working on. They still needed a lot of work, but he was determined to fix them.

Laying out on one of the lounge chairs, my heart sped up when the music blaring from his garage came to a complete halt. That meant he was wrapping it up. I'd come to learn his routine the past few days. At first, I half expected his house to be overrun by his friends, but no one came by. He was solitary and a creature of habit, just like me.

All too soon, the gate to the pool area opened and he walked through, rubbing a towel across his forehead. He hadn't noticed me yet, but when he did, he stopped and a small smirk tilted up the corner of his lips. "What's up, buttercup?"

Okay. Not quite the reaction I was going for, but at least I have his attention. I actually missed our bantering back and forth, but I wasn't going to tell him that. I got up from the chair and walked toward him, making sure to put a little extra sway to my hips. "I was wondering if you'd be up for a little competition? You know, to get the blood flowing and all. I need a pick-me-up."

"You don't say. I'm intrigued. What type of competition are you suggesting?" He smiled and I heard a hint of the old Pax, the one who wanted to devour my body.

I stopped in front of him and tilted my head, making sure to touch him when I said, "A race. First one to swim the length of the pool, wins."

Before he answered, he unbuttoned his jeans and let them fall to the ground. Clad in his boxers, he smirked. "Last one in is a rotten egg." He slapped me on the ass and dove into the pool.

I didn't think twice. I jumped. The water was a little cool, but it felt good on my heated skin. Paxton waited for me at the other end and when I got there he looked at me over his shoulder.

"What do I get if I win?"

My pulse quickened and my breaths came out in rapid pants. I was competitive by nature, but even I knew there was no way I could win against him. I should have thought this through better. "You can kiss me."

His eyebrows shot up. "And what do you get if you win?"

I hesitated and settled on something non-committal. "Breakfast in bed."

He seemed a little put off by my request, but shook it off and nodded. "It's a deal."

If I was truthful with myself, I wanted to lose. Licking my lips, I kept my gaze on the other side of the pool, the finish line.

"All right. One . . . two . . . three . . . *go*."

As fast as I could, I pumped my arms and my legs until they burned. His pool was Olympic sized so it was about twice the length of a normal pool. I didn't even look at his progress, I just kept going, breathing in gulps of air every few strokes.

When I stopped hearing his arms and legs pounding against the water I knew it was done. He was already at the other end waiting on me. Gasping for air, I held onto the edge of the pool and leaned my forehead against it. I hated to lose.

"You lost, sunshine."

"No shit," I growled.

"I need you to turn around." His voice was right by my ear and I could feel the heat of his body behind me.

Lifting my head, I huffed and turned around, my back to the pool wall. His arms closed me in. "I guess you're going to want payment," I whispered, looking down at his lips.

Pressing his body to mine, he grabbed my thighs and lifted me up. I was straddling his waist, but now I had to hold onto him. Almost hesitantly, I wrapped my arms around his neck and tried desperately to breathe without him knowing how bad he affected me.

"I did win fair and square," he pointed out. A mischievous smirk splayed across his face.

"A deal's a deal. You, Mr. Emerson, get to kiss me." I said, trying not to look too excited.

His whole body scorched me with every single touch on my bare skin. His hands were tight under my ass, holding me in place. I was on fire and I wanted more. Between his legs, his cock was hard and pushed into me when he backed me into the wall. I throbbed and ached with the need to move against him, to feel him inside me. He hovered by my face, so close I could hear him breathing hard through his nose. Our gazes locked with half-lidded stares. And . . . that was it. He never brought his lips to mine.

I was going to lose it. "What's wrong? Don't you want to kiss me?"

He looked hurt and frankly, a little angry. Pulling back, he let me go and moved away from me. The ever growing distance between us growing with each second. "Nah. I told you I wouldn't ask for anything you weren't willing to give. I have to go," he said, getting out of the pool. "There's somewhere I need to be." Once out, he quickly headed for the door.

"Pax," I called. He kept going. *But I am willing to give it to you.* I almost said it out loud, but it was too late. He'd already walked through the patio door.

Slamming the door shut, I watched him disappear up the stairs. Shit. Had I hurt him in some way? Well, I wasn't going to let him ignore me anymore. Whatever was so important that he had to leave me for, I was going to find out. It might be a little stalkerish, but I wasn't going to sit by myself another night longer.

CHAPTER 8

Gabriella

I HAD NO clue how I was going to find out where Paxton was going until my saving grace came in the form of a phone call. My bedroom was just across from his and when I heard him talking, I edged toward the door and listened in.

"Fuck yeah, I'm gonna be there. Everything's all ready," he said low. What was he talking about? I wish I knew who the other person was and what they were saying.

"Okay, meet me at Delaney's track in about an hour. I don't know if I'm going to the club tonight, but I'll let you know."

As soon as he hung up the phone, I tiptoed back to my room and gently shut the door. What the hell was

Delaney's track? Searching through my phone, I found an address for it, but not a website. It was only ten miles away. What could he possibly be doing there? He was the one who wanted me to stay here with him and now he was acting like I didn't exist? *I don't think so.* Whatever he was doing, I was going to find out. This shit was ending tonight.

Paxton's footsteps thundered across the floor on down the steps until they completely went silent once the front door shut. Quickly, I threw on my jeans and tank top and ran my hands through my hair. How the hell did I fall so low as to resort to stalking? Ashleigh would get a kick out of this if she knew what I was doing.

The sound of a revving engine and squealing tires caught my attention, but I didn't get to the window fast enough to see him leave. I did, however, see the tire tracks on the driveway. Thankfully, the Hummer was still there which meant I had access to a vehicle. Rushing down the stairs, I bounded out of the house and made sure to lock the door. Paxton had a habit of not locking the doors. That had to be a man thing, because Bradley was the same way.

With the address in the GPS, I was ready to go. Apparently, I had to go right by my apartment which was good considering I needed to check my mail anyway. When I got there, I quickly opened my little mailbox, and of course, it was full of junk. Still, if I didn't get all that crap out, my mailman would just shove more and more in until I couldn't get any of it out. Since I had about twenty minutes to spare, I parked and raced up the stairs to my apartment to use the bathroom. I was actually nervous, which wasn't normal for me.

Bolting up the steps, I took two at a time and had my

keys ready to unlock the door. I stopped dead in my tracks and choked when I noticed not one, but two black roses by my doorstep. *You have got to be kidding me.* Hesitantly, I took in my surroundings and didn't notice anything else amiss. There was a note attached to the roses just like the other day. From the looks of them, they'd been left there for a while. I hadn't been by in three days.

Gently, I picked them up and unlocked my door, opening it wide. The other black rose was still on my counter, dried out and shriveled with the note I left beside it. I opened up the new note.

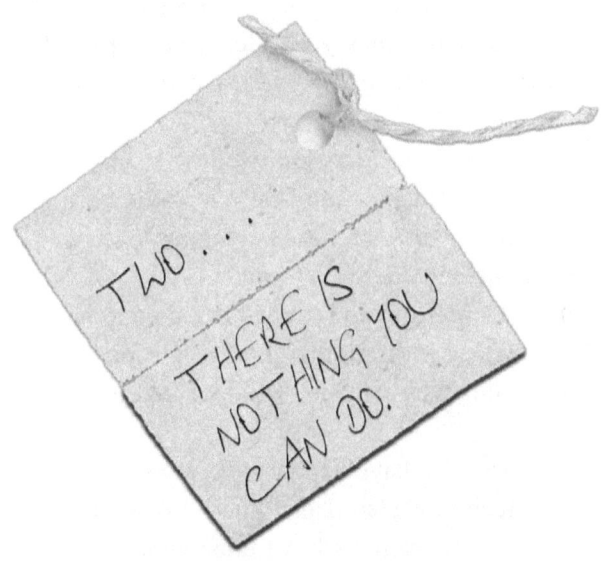

This shit was getting beyond weird. Sliding my phone out of my back pocket, I dialed up Ryley's number. Luckily, he answered on the second ring. The last thing I wanted to do was worry Ashleigh when she needed to stay calm for the babies.

"Hey, what's up?" he answered.

I threw the roses in the trash and held both notes in my hand. "I don't know, but whatever it is, I don't like it."

"What's wrong?" he asked, concern etched in his voice.

"I've been getting flowers at my apartment. Today is the second time they were left on my doorstep."

"Oh, is that it? It's probably your douchebag ex wanting you back. Why don't you tell him to fuck off?"

Sitting down on the couch, I sighed and peered down at the two pieces of paper. "Well, it's probably because it's not him. Bradley isn't the type to leave *black* roses."

"Black? Who the hell would leave you black flowers? Was there a note?"

I nodded like an idiot knowing he couldn't see me. "Two of them, actually. The first one came with a single black rose. It said one is for the beginning."

"What the hell does that mean?"

"How the hell should I know? But then today, I found two black roses with another note. This one said, two, there is nothing you can do. Kind of creepy if you ask me."

"Shit. And you have no idea who it could be?"

"I'm clueless, Ryley. I just know I don't like it. I get that weird spidery feeling when I think about it."

"Where's Paxton? Ashleigh told me about you staying with him. Is he there?"

"No, he hasn't been spending much time with me. I guess pushing him away finally worked." Over the past three days I'd been nearly nonexistent to him, until today when he raced me in the pool.

"And you of all people should know how that works out," he snapped. "Do you remember when you bitched me out for doing that to Ashleigh?"

I remembered that day very well. I hated watching her suffer because of what he was putting her through. "Yes," I answered reluctantly.

"Well, the guy likes you, Gabby. Yes, he pissed me off by taking you and Ashleigh to the Dark Side, but if he didn't I don't know what I would've done if you guys weren't there. The guy's probably just done with being turned down. It sounds to me like you're going to have to make the first move. Any man in their right mind would be gun-shy by now. Shit, you've turned him down how many times? A hundred and seventy-three?"

"You know why I won't do that, Ryley."

He scoffed. "That's bullshit and you know it. I think you're just afraid, so stop making up excuses. But on to more important things . . . whatever you do, don't go to your apartment without someone with you. If you get anymore notes, you might seriously need to go to the police. Or better yet, get your brother to call Mason. He'll know what to do."

Mason was my brother's friend and my stand in coach when he couldn't make it. He was an MMA fighter and an undercover detective. With his amazing skills, he busted a whole underground fighting ring last year after several fighters lost their lives. He was a legend in the UFC community.

"If I get anymore letters I'll call Mason myself," I promised. "I've wanted to talk to Paxton about it, but we haven't really had the chance to talk with his newfound busy schedule."

"Well, make him listen," he shouted. "All you have to do is make the first move. I promise."

"Okay, I'm going to him now. It's probably nothing to be worried about." Getting up from the couch, I shoved the notes in my back pocket and started for the door.

"Just keep me updated, Gabby. And stay out of trouble."

"Will do. I'll talk to you soon." We said our goodbyes and I rushed out of my apartment and down to the car.

My heart was on overdrive the whole way to the track, and thankfully, I made it there without having a heart attack. There were cars everywhere, especially race cars. You had to pay to park, so I gave the man my money and found a parking place amongst the drunken patrons. *Great.* I wasn't in the mood for problems.

Once parked, I hopped out of the Hummer and started on my way, not paying attention to anyone as I passed by. "Hey baby, you alone tonight? I'd be happy to give you a *ride.*"

Biting my tongue, I kept going, but the idiot wouldn't stop. "I see we're playing hard to get. I told you I'd give a ride tonight, sugar lips. What ya say?" He grabbed his crotch and nodded at me.

"I say go fuck yourself, dickhead. I'd rather my dildo give me a ride."

Shouts of laughter sounded behind me, along with the snarls of the man I just told to fuck off. He called me a "no good, stupid cunt" and I replied with a finger in the air. Why men thought that kind of shit would help them get a piece of ass was beyond me. I guess some women liked the disgusting pick up lines.

The track was huge and I had no clue where to find Paxton. In the middle, there were cars getting ready to race and some that had just gotten done racing. There were people everywhere in the stands, so I searched through the crowd until I found an open section. To my luck, there was a spot right near the front. Once I was seated, there was one person I recognized coming down the steps toward my section. When his head lifted, he spotted me almost immediately and smiled.

Sliding past the people on our row, he sat down beside me with a beer in hand. The baseball cap covering his head hung low over his eyes, but not so much that I couldn't recognize him.

"Gabriella," he greeted with a nod.

"Cliff," I replied back. "So we meet again."

"I must admit, I didn't peg you for a racing type of girl."

I snorted. "You'd be surprised the types of things I do. I'm not taking someone else's seat am I? I just got here and I didn't know where to go."

He shook his head. "No, not at all. Who are you here with?"

Behind him, I scanned the crowd to see if I could find Paxton but I couldn't see him anywhere. "I'm kind of by myself, but I'm looking for someone. I know he's here."

"Your boyfriend?"

"No, definitely not. His name is Paxton."

Cliff snorted and gestured toward the center of the track. "If you happen to be talking about Paxton Emerson, he's out there about to race."

Eyes wide, I followed his line of sight until I saw him, leaned up against a bright blue Acura NSX. "He races? I didn't know that."

"Oh, yeah, he's one of the best out there. I also heard he's some kind of champion MMA fighter. I don't keep up with that sport, so I have no clue who he is. I'm more of a football type of guy." The thought made me laugh. "What's so funny?" he asked, grinning at me.

"I guess it would probably shock you to know that I'm an MMA fighter too."

Chuckling, he took another gulp of his beer and set it down, clearly not believing me. When he noticed I wasn't laughing, his smile turned sheepish. "You're shitting me, right? You're sexy as fuck. How could you be a *fighter*?"

"Hey, I'm not the only one. There are other women fighters who are hot." I slid my phone out of my back pocket and showed him the promotional picture of me and Jaden Eller before our last fight.

His eyes went wide. "Holy shit. That really is you. Damn, I never would've thought it."

I put my phone back and giggled. "It's new for me. I just started this year. My brother was the Heavyweight champ for a while. Now he's retired and he coaches me."

"Well, then it looks like I'm sitting beside MMA royalty over here. I'm honored," he said, bumping me in the shoulder.

I rolled my eyes. "Oh, whatever. Most people who know me would say I'm a royal pain in the ass. So, tell me about Paxton. If you just moved here how do you know he's one of the best?"

Picking his beer back up, he kept his gaze on Paxton. "He's been here the past couple of nights. I've watched him race. I heard by one of our other neighbors that this place was pretty tight. I'd love to be out there racing, but with me trying to get onto the force, I don't have the time for it."

Speaking of talking to neighbors, I wanted to ask him about the roses to see if he saw the person who put them on my doorstep. Before I could do that, he patted me on the knee and pointed to the track. "He's up."

Turning my attention to the cars, Paxton was strapped in his Acura and getting into place along with several other drivers. "How many laps do they have to do?"

"Just three if you go by the last couple of nights. I guess it's because they have so many people racing. Your boy is in one of the advanced groups."

No wonder he was able to keep up with me in the go kart race. He had his own experience racing. *Sly bastard.* The track wasn't just shaped like an oval. It actually had twists and turns, but it was very tight. There wasn't much room for error.

Once the flag went down, they were off, the sounds of their motors revving echoed in my ears. Paxton was neck and neck with another driver, but then a third one came up and tried to sneak in between them. The excitement had my adrenaline pumping. So this was what he was doing the past three nights. I was starting to feel a little better about his intentions on going out.

One lap down and two more to go. He was in the lead and gaining distance. He took the turns with ease, just like he did on the go karts.

"So what's going on with you and Paxton?" Cliff asked. "You said he's not your boyfriend and you had no idea he raced, but yet you're here to watch him."

I snorted. "I guess you can say I kind of lost a bet and I'm paying him back. It's really hard to explain."

Paxton was on his third lap and almost to the finish line. Getting to my feet, I watched in complete and utter amazement as he zipped by and crossed the finish line, the checkered flag waving rapidly in the air. Cliff stood and joined me as I jumped up and down, screaming Paxton's name. I can't believe he didn't tell me he raced.

Paxton leapt out of his car and a swarm of people rushed up to him, giving him high fives and congratulating him. It was all great until a tall blonde jumped in his arms and hugged him around the neck. I'd never personally seen him with a female other than Kacey. The smile he gave her wasn't his normal smile either. Who the hell was she?

My gut clenched and I realized for the first time, I didn't like other women talking to him, or touching him. I had no right to be jealous, but I was. "Who's that down there with him? Has she been here the past few nights?"

Cliff furrowed his brows and turned to look. "Oh yeah, I've seen her here. She's with your boy's crowd." With narrowed eyes, he glanced back at me. "Why do you want to know?"

I waved him off. "No reason, she just looks like someone I might know. I think I'm going to head out though. Do you mind walking me to my car? I had a little bit of trouble coming in and the last thing I want is to have to kick some fucktard's ass."

"As much as I'd like to see that, I think I can handle it myself. Why don't we go get some coffee? There's a place right up the street from our apartment . . ."

"Macie's café?" I blurted out.

He chuckled and nodded. "I have to be at the station early in the morning, so I figured coffee would be the better alternative for tonight."

We started up the stands and I couldn't help but look back at Paxton and the blonde, celebrating his win. I guess he was over wanting to be with me, and I quickly realized how much I hated it.

I turned my attention back to Cliff. "Oh yeah, that's right. How's the training going? Do you think you'll make the squad?"

He shrugged. "I don't know, but I think I have a fighting chance. Do you want to just meet me at the café?"

"Yes, let's do that. There's actually something I wanted to talk to you about."

He walked me to the Hummer and then left to find his car. It felt wrong to get coffee with him, but if I wasn't going to be home for the next week or so, I needed a pair of eyes to keep watch.

Cliff and I both grabbed a coffee and I snatched up a pumpkin muffin. Ever since I'd been at Paxton's house I hadn't had one. We decided to sit outside at their iron wrought tables since they were about to close up.

"So what did you want to talk about?" Cliff asked.

"Have you seen anyone near my apartment? Like maybe someone who came by and left some flowers on my doorstep?"

Shaking his head, he took a sip of his coffee. "No, but I did see them in front of your door. I was tempted to take them away. I thought it might be your ex wanting you back."

"Why were you wanting to take them away?" I asked, laughing.

His brown eyes bore into mine, all serious. "Because I thought that if you didn't get back with your ex, I might be able to ask you out."

"Really? Oh, wow." I shoved a bite of my muffin in my mouth, not knowing what to say. He was hot as hell, but he wasn't Paxton. "So you didn't see the person who left them?"

"No, but I can keep a look out for you. Are you worried about something?"

Looking down at my coffee, I didn't really know how to explain it. It was just a feeling I had when I read the note. "I'm not sure yet. I know it wasn't my ex who put them there and other than that, I don't know of anyone who would've done it."

"What about Paxton? Could it be him?"

"I know for a fact it's not."

"And how do you know that?"

"I just do." Reaching into my purse, I pulled out a pen and grabbed a napkin on the table. "I'm going to give you my number. If you see anyone at my door, I want you to call me." I wrote my number down and passed it to him.

"You know, I have some friends at the station who owe me a favor. I could get them to run the prints on the letters, if there's any on them that is."

"Really?" I asked, wide-eyed. "You'd do that? I didn't really want to go to the police about this, but if you think it would help that'd be great." The notes were in my back pocket so I pulled them out and handed them to him.

He stared down at them. "It'll probably take a couple

of days, but I'll see what they can do."

Sitting back in my chair, I sighed and took a sip of my coffee. "Thank you. I appreciate you doing this for me."

About that time, something caught the corner of my eye. I squinted and focused my attention on the blue sports car headed our way.

Cliff sat back in his chair and put the notes in his pocket with an amused smirk on his face. "It looks like your boyfriend found you," he quipped, taking another sip of his coffee.

Paxton obviously didn't know I was with someone else because when he saw Cliff, his expression went from passive to livid. Slamming on the brakes, he got out of the car and glared at us.

"He's not my boyfriend," I said as I got to my feet. He sure as hell was acting like it though. "What are you doing?" I asked incredulously.

His nostrils flared. "I could ask you the same thing. Whoever that is, say goodnight. The date's over." Cliff chuckled, drawing both mine and Paxton's attention. Paxton clearly wasn't in the mood to be provoked. "Is there a problem?"

Smirking, Cliff gestured toward us both and shook his head. "No, I'm just curious to see how she handles this. Gabriella doesn't seem like the type of girl to put up with someone telling her what to do."

"Oh, so you know her now?" Paxton growled. "Who the fuck are you?"

His anger and possessiveness was turning me on. Hot damn, he was sexy when that little vein bulged on his forehead.

Cliff didn't move an inch. He stayed perfectly comfortable in his chair. "I'm her neighbor. And yes, I'd say I'm getting to know her quite well."

Paxton stepped forward, but I blocked him and put a hand on his chest. "Pax, stop. You're acting like an idiot. Why do you even care? I thought you were over me. Cliff's my friend and has been kind enough to help me out with something." I glared up at him and hissed. "Why don't you just go back to your blonde from the track?"

His scowl turned into a mask of confusion. "What are you talking about? Is that jealousy I hear in your voice?"

"Don't flatter yourself. I think you need to leave. I'll be back when I feel like it."

"Sorry, but that's not going to happen," he said grabbing my hand. "You made a deal and you're going to keep it." He pulled me toward his car and when I looked back, Cliff got up from the table, his smile gone.

"I don't think I'd do that if I were you," he warned. Slowly, Cliff reached behind his back and my eyes went wide. Was he reaching for a fucking gun?

Paxton stopped, but he didn't let me go. "Gabby, so help me God, either get in my car now, or get in the Hummer and follow me home. I don't want this night to get ugly."

"Then put the testosterone away and let me handle this." Reluctantly, he let me go and walked back to his car, keeping his venomous stare on Cliff.

Cliff never took his eyes away from Paxton, even when I was safely away. "Please tell me you're not going back to his place. I can take you to your apartment if you need me to. I'm not scared of that fucker."

Sighing, I grabbed my purse and faced him. Now that

Pax wasn't hiding his feelings, the tension between us had come to a breaking point and it was about to explode. It was time to let it.

"I'm not going back to my apartment, Cliff."

He scoffed. "You can't be fucking serious. I never thought you'd let someone talk to you like that."

"Trust me, I don't. He's going to get an earful when we get back."

"Why do you have to go with him at all?"

I chuckled, but he didn't see the humor in it. "It's complicated. I honestly can't explain any more than that. But if you would, please call me if you see or hear anything."

He nodded and huffed. "All right, I'll call. Are you sure you're going to be okay? You're not being forced into anything are you? You can tell me and I'll get you out of here."

Pax wouldn't have to force me to do anything. I couldn't wait to get back to his place. First, I would give him a piece of my mind. Then, I'd give him a piece of something else. "No, he's not forcing me. Believe me, this is something I want to do. I made a deal and I won't break it."

Clenching his jaw, he sneered at Paxton over my shoulder before turning back to me. "Well, if that's what you have to do, I can't stop you. Just be careful."

"I'll be okay. I promise. Besides, I can handle myself."

A gleam twinkled in his eye. "So I can tell. I'll keep in touch." Turning on his heel, he looked back at me once and smiled before getting into his truck. I didn't even bother looking at Paxton when I got in his Hummer because I knew he was fuming. Quickly, I started up the car and headed on my way to his house with him close behind.

I couldn't take it anymore. His open jealousy had shown me a glimpse of how he really feels. And my flimsy excuses were no longer enough to hide behind. My brother would be disappointed in me, but what else could I do?

CHAPTER 9

Gabriella

AS SOON AS I pulled into his driveway, I quickly jumped out of his car and headed into the house. I couldn't wait any longer.

"*Gabriella*," he shouted, racing to catch up. "She's my cousin," he yelled. "Do you remember my Aunt Jackie? April's her daughter. My uncle owns the track. *Gabby*, wait up."

He thought I was mad. I *had* been jealous, but it didn't matter right now. He didn't know what was coming next, but it was inevitable—like the tide, or the sunrise.

I leapt up the steps two at a time; Pax hot on my heels. Walking right through the door, I stopped a few feet into the room, threw my purse on the floor and turned to watch him enter.

"Look, I'm sorry," he began, but stopped when he saw me just standing there, arms at my sides, breathing heavy.

Our eyes locked and just as he was about to continue talking, I closed the distance between us, shoving him against the wall. Pushing my tongue inside his mouth, I felt the fire instantly blaze between us. It took him a split second to catch up to the moment, but then his hands snaked around my waist, pulling me in tight—his grip almost bruising.

"Fuck," he growled into my mouth.

Nothing in that moment mattered other than the feel of his warm, large hands caressing me feverishly. It was almost as if we were starved for each other and not able to get enough. I honestly didn't think I'd ever quench my thirst for him. I'd fought it for so long, I almost felt like a ravenous beast.

Paxton turned us, slamming my back into the wall. I wrapped my legs around his waist and began moving against him, his cock growing rapidly against my core. I grabbed my shirt and ripped it over my head. Groaning, he sucked and nipped the top of my breast before he stopped and looked up at me. I bit my lip and smiled.

He shook his head and smirked, leaning in to devour my mouth. Grabbing my ass, he held me in place as he stood up straight and made his way up the stairs, never breaking his lips from mine. Bumping into a few walls, we finally made it to our destination.

We fell onto his bed. It smelled just like him. "I want you so bad," I mumbled against his mouth, moving my hips in circles under his weight.

He unclasped my bra with one hand. Once I was free,

he closed his lips over a nipple and sucked, pulling and biting it until I screamed out. I cried in pleasure as he massaged and kissed every square inch of my breasts, fondling my nipples with his tongue. My underwear was soaked and even more so when he bit my tender flesh. The pain of it felt so damn good.

Sliding his lips up my neck to my cheek, he closed them over my lips. "And I've wanted you," he murmured low. "Fuck, you have no idea how bad."

I grabbed his hand and slid it down under the waistband of my jeans. Using my hand to push his against my wet heat, I moaned. "Oh, I think I have an idea of how bad."

"Fuck me. I can't wait anymore." He pulled his hand out and worked on unbuttoning my jeans. As soon as he was done, we worked together to push them down enough to where I could kick them off.

Crawling backward, he caressed his fingers down my legs until he was completely off the bed. Never taking his gaze off of mine, he lifted his shirt over his head and unbuttoned his jeans, letting them fall to the floor. His cock bulged behind his boxers and I bit my lip as he rubbed his arousal through the material. Slowly, he slid his boxers down and smirked as he gave himself a few pumps up and down this length. He watched me watch him and it was the single most erotic thing I'd ever seen.

"Come here." I touched myself over my wet panties, needing him *now*.

Pax wasted no time and crawled on the bed. I slid my underwear off and threw it across the room, opening wide for him. His tongue trailed up my inner thigh and passed over my clit with one quick flick. My body jerked and the feel of his breath as he chuckled, made my toes curl. It was so hot hearing his satisfaction.

Delving deep, he buried his tongue inside me and swirled it around, fucking me. His tongue was so warm and needy as he tasted me, driving me to the edge. My clit ached for release and when he pulled his tongue out and started sucking on it, my body exploded. Fisting my hands in his dark hair, I screamed out my pleasure. He slowly lowered his pace and licked me as my body shook, tasting my desire for him.

When I looked down, his green eyes blazed with an intensity that made me tremble. I'd never seen anyone stare at me like that. It was kind of scary, but in a good, primal way . . . almost possessively. Covering me with his body, I could feel the tip of him at my opening. I wanted him to push in so fucking bad. Instead, he closed his lips over mine and grabbed a hold of my face, kissing me deeply. I tasted myself on his lips.

His tip pushed in a little and I moaned, biting his bottom lip. "Just do it. I want you. I want to feel all of you."

Growling deep in his chest, he plunged in as far as he could go. I screamed and dug my nails into his back as he rocked me back and forth, hard. My core stretched to fit all of him, but the pain of it made my eyes water. It hurt, but it felt so fucking good.

Pax found a spot behind my ear and bit down, sending chills cascading down my body. What made it even better was that he didn't stop there. Down my neck and across my collarbone, he nipped and sucked his way until he reached my nipples. As hard as he could, he took my nipple in his mouth and pulled with his lips, flicking his tongue across my swollen peaks.

Another orgasm built between my legs and judging by his strangled groan he knew I was about to come. Instead of leaving me on my back, he wrapped his arms around me and lifted me up on his lap. We were sitting up on his bed with me on top of him. He was in so deep.

"Ride me," he commanded, never taking his mouth away from my nipple.

Lifting my hips, I sat down on him until I got a good rhythm. My body clenched and I was so close. Paxton was too by the way his cock pulsated inside me. "I'm going to come," I warned.

"Keep going, baby. I want to come inside you."

My eyes rolled into the back of my head and my insides tightened. Just the thought of him releasing inside me sent me over the edge. "*Yes*," I cried breathlessly. His fingers dug into my hips and he held me down on his cock as we both reached our climax, our bodies melding together. I could feel his release as he came inside me, all hot and primal as he yelled out, his body jerking in spasms. Laying my head on his shoulder, my heart beat out of control.

Paxton lowered me to the bed and gently pulled out before resting behind me with his arm across my stomach. "No regrets?" he asked.

I shook my head and nuzzled closer to him. "None," I answered softly.

"So tomorrow morning, you're not going to sneak away?"

Laughing, I turned my face to the side so I could see him. "I'm not going anywhere. I promise."

Taking my chin, he held me firm and kissed me. "Good, because I'm not letting you go. That's a promise."

Hopefully, it was a promise he could keep.

CHAPTER 10

Gabriella

WHEN HE ASKED me if I was going to sneak away, I should've asked him the same question. I was expecting him to be in bed with me when the sun rose, but needless to say, he wasn't. It was seven o'clock in the morning. Where was he?

Climbing out of bed, I grabbed my clothes up off the floor and rushed across the hall to my room so I could grab a quick shower and get a change of clothes. After sliding on a pair of yoga pants and a tank top, I heard a noise outside and peered out the window; the light to Paxton's garage was on.

He didn't regret last night, did he? Before getting the courage to go out there, I trudged into the kitchen and brewed a cup of coffee. If anything were to go downhill, I could count on my coffee to keep me sane. Once it was done, I carried the mug outside and slowly made my way to his garage. He had the music on, but it wasn't loud enough to hear clearly outside the building walls.

One of the doors was open, so I peeked inside and watched him as he worked on one of the old cars. Dressed in a pair of holey jeans with no shirt on, my whole body tingled in anticipation. Even though I was a little sore, I wanted him again. He could be sweaty and covered in grease and I wouldn't care. Everything inside me craved him. I'd denied myself for so long, it felt like I'd never be able to catch up. It was exciting.

I had to tighten my legs together to help subdue the ache between my thighs. The way he stared at his work with such pride and contentment helped me see a whole new side of him I'd never seen before. How could I not see that there was more to him than he led on? *It's because I didn't want to see it.*

"I know you're there, sunshine," he quipped. "I'm sure you can admire me much better from in here."

Rolling my eyes, I chuckled and walked through the door. "How did you know I was there? There's no way you could've seen me."

Wiping his hands on a towel, he finally looked over at me and smiled. "I don't know, I can just tell when you're near. It used to drive me crazy at the gym."

I walked past him to a desk in the corner and sat down. "Trust me, it used to do the same thing to me." Paxton went back to working on his car while I looked around his garage. Across the whole back wall there were frames with before and after pictures in them, of cars that were junk before and then completely restored. They didn't even look like the same vehicles.

"Did you do all of these?" I asked incredulously.

Over my shoulder, he kept his attention on the car motor and grinned. "Does that surprise you? I told you there was more to me than just fighting. I do enjoy other things in life. Which I'm sure you happened to have witnessed last night."

Smiling, I turned back to the photos. "Well . . . I might have forgotten. Do you care to refresh my memory?"

All too soon, he came up behind me and put his arms around my waist. His breath tickled my neck as he leaned down and kissed me, his cock hard against my back. "I'd be more than happy to. I'm sorry I wasn't in bed this morning. I couldn't sleep."

"Why not?"

His hands lifted to my breasts and he squeezed, massaging them. "Because I couldn't be beside you without wanting to fuck you. It was like I took a whole bottle of fucking Viagra."

"Oh my God, why didn't you wake me up?"

His lips touched my shoulder and worked their way up to my cheek. "You needed your rest. Besides, I know you were sore last night after we got done. I'm sorry if I hurt you."

"Pax, you have nothing to—" Something on his wall caught my undivided attention. It was the last frame and there inside was a picture of my brother's old Ford Bronco. The first picture was of it with the faded blue paint, busted wheels, and raggedy convertible top. Matt drove that thing until it was falling apart.

However, the second picture was of it fully restored

to what it was today. The metallic blue paint was shiny, not dull. The top was a crisp white, instead of dingy yellow, and the wheels were a lot larger now with a set of bad ass custom made chrome rims. *How is this possible?*

Furrowing my brows, I turned around in his arms. "Why do you have pictures of my brother's car? I rode around in that thing for years. He had it fixed up years ago. I'd know it from anywhere."

"Yes, I know. For the longest time, I thought you would remember me when I started going to Carter's gym, but you never did."

"I don't understand. What are you talking about? I thought you hated my brother?" Paxton was a part of Kyle's crowd and everyone in that group hated my brother, Tyler, and all of their friends. It was just the way it was.

Taking my hand, Paxton walked me back to the desk and I sat down while he finished up with what he was doing. "Gabby, I've never hated your brother. Every time I tried to tell you the truth you basically slammed a door in my face. You automatically assumed I was just like Kyle."

"But you were," I blurted out. "You've gotten in so much trouble over the years, Pax. You had a reputation and it wasn't a good one."

He sighed. "Yes, I know, but it was never for things like Kyle did. A few drunken brawls and whatnot, yes, but never the stuff that bastard did. I met your brother before all of that happened. It was before I really got into the whole fighting scene."

"Was that when you were dating Kacey?"

"No, we had already split ways at that time. I remember you though. You were in high school. I came by your house to talk to Matt about ideas I had for his car, when I saw you on the track, racing your go kart. Your brother and I talked the whole time you were out there and I couldn't take my eyes off of you. If you weren't still in high school I would've asked you out."

I tried to think back to those days but I couldn't place him at all. "Damn, grandpa. How much older than me are you?" I was only twenty-three, but my birthday was in December, a little over three months away.

"I'm twenty-eight," he replied, lifting a brow daring me to comment.

"How come I don't remember you? Did we meet?"

He snorted. "Yes. You were with a group of your friends so it doesn't surprise me you didn't notice me. Judging by the guys you were around, I wasn't your type."

To be honest, it wasn't the type of guys I would've chosen for myself, but I wanted to be a part of the crowd and those were the people I needed to be around. The girls were stuck up bitches, but I tolerated them just to be part of the group.

"Besides," Paxton continued, "I didn't exactly look like I do now. Back then, I had blond hair and I wasn't as built. I guess the muscles and the tattoos got your attention."

There was a greasy rag on his desk so I picked it up and threw it at him. "Actually, smart ass, it was your sexy green eyes that got me. The tattoos and muscles were only a bonus."

He looked back at me and winked. "So anyway, back to the main part of the story. Your brother came into the garage wanting someone to restore his car. Since it was my area of expertise, I took on the project."

"How did you get the knowledge to do that? Was it

from your uncle who owns the race track?"

His lip titled up in a sad smile, but kept his focus on the engine as he worked. "Yeah, I kind of grew up around cars and racing. The whole fighting thing came later. So with that being said, at this point in time I was friends with Kyle, but it was before I got into all my trouble. That all came later, and even then I never did anything to your brother. He knows this. I was out of Kyle's group before all of that took place."

Mouth gaping open, I stared at him in horror. I'd never asked my brother about Paxton because I always assumed he was one of the bad guys. I didn't have a reason to think otherwise. All this time, I treated Paxton like shit when he had nothing to do with Kyle's deceitful attempts to fuck over my brother.

"And you tried to tell me numerous times," I stated sadly.

Paxton shrugged and backed away from the car, wiping his hands on his towel. "It's not like it mattered anyway. You were too busy with college and your dickwad boyfriend to notice me."

"Oh, let's be clear. I noticed you," I confessed. "I hated myself for it, but I wanted you bad. I just assumed you were part of the plot to sabotage my brother, so I had to hate you. I felt like a traitor being attracted to you."

"And now?" he asked, peering over at me.

Getting to my feet, I slowly walked over to him and put my arms around his shoulders. "Now I just feel like a coldhearted bitch. I thought you pursued me just to get a rise out of my brother. That's why Tyler came after you so hard because I told him that's probably what you were doing."

He put his arms around my waist and chuckled. "Yeah, Tyler and I are never going to be besties—there's too much history. And, your brother might not like us to-gether, but I know he doesn't hate me. We actually talked that night while you were helping Kacey bind up her wrists."

"I'm sorry," I murmured. "Ashleigh told me to stop pushing you away and when you basically stopped caring if I came or went, I thought I was too late."

A sly smile spread across his face. "I had to do some-thing to get your attention. Besides, I needed you to come to me. I wasn't going to ask for anything you didn't want to give."

Smacking him in the arm, I narrowed my eyes. "So it was just to pay me back? Well I gotta tell you, it worked. I was so pissed at you, especially when you left me in the pool." And we still hadn't talked about what happened with Cliff. He hadn't brought it up, but he needed to know that nothing was going on other than wanting his help.

Paxton leaned down and kissed me, holding me close to his body. I didn't want to break the contact, but I had no choice. "Pax," I whispered, breaking the trance. "I need to talk to you about last night. About Cliff."

Clenching his teeth, he huffed and tilted his head back. "Why do we have to talk about that barnacle now? It's obvious the dude's hard up for you. And what's worse, he's your fucking neighbor."

"A barnacle?"

"He's one of those guys who's going to attach him-self to you. Wait and see. He's a creep, I know it."

Laughing, I rolled my eyes. "Not to give you a guilt trip, but he's kind of helping me out with something. I wanted to talk to you about it, but we weren't necessarily talking at the time. I didn't know what else to do."

Paxton furrowed his brows and stepped back. "What's going on?"

Sighing, I leaned against his desk and crossed my arms across my chest while he waited, concern etched in his gaze. "Okay, first, let me explain something to you. Cliff is my neighbor. He's ex military and he's about to be a cop with the LAPD."

"Great, give the boy a fucking medal," he grumbled.

Ignoring his comment, I sighed and kept going. "Anyway, when I went to my apartment at the beginning of the week, I had a flower by my doorstep."

Paxton's gaze grew dark. "Who was it from? Him?"

"No," I blurted. "It wasn't him. At first, I wondered if it could be Bradley, but then when I got a closer look I realized there was no way."

"Why is that?"

"It was black, Pax. The rose was *black*. I've never known a guy to send a black rose to a girl. And the note was kind of cryptic. Well, both of the notes were."

"You got more than one? What did they say?" he questioned, eyes wide.

I told him and he didn't like it at all. At first, I thought he would be flippant about it and brush it off as some kind of joke, but he took it the way I did. It was a little creepy and I wasn't going to lie, it kind of scared me.

"So where does Cliff come into all of this?"

"He took the letters to see if they can get prints off of them. Plus, he's going to call me if I have any more deliveries. All of this happened this week, so I'm assuming it's going to happen again soon. I just don't know how far this person is willing to go."

Paxton reached for me and pulled me into his arms. "Whatever you do, don't go to your apartment by yourself. Whoever this person is, they know where you live. Do not go there unless someone else is with you."

Breathing him in, I laid my head on his chest and closed my eyes. "I won't."

"I'll do what I have to do to keep you safe. I can promise you that."

"And you always keep your promises, right?" I teased.

He kissed the top of my head. "You're damn right. I'm not going to let anything happen to you."

To get my mind off of black flowers and feelings of doom, I lowered my hand and rubbed him through his jeans.

Groaning, he lowered his mouth to my neck and bit down. "You're killing me, sunshine. I wouldn't start something you can't finish."

I scoffed. "Who said I can't finish it?"

Sliding my yoga pants and underwear to the floor, I stepped out of them and lifted my tank top over my head. Paxton raked his gaze down my body and licked his lips. "You're honestly trying to kill me." He picked me up in his arms and slammed me down on the hood of one of his cars. I yelped when I felt the hood dent with my weight.

He laughed and lowered his jeans to the floor. "Don't worry about it, sunshine. Every time I look at this car, I'm going to remember I fucked you on it."

Grabbing my thighs, he pulled me down to the edge of the car and I wrapped my legs around him, ready for him to take me. He plunged inside and reached behind me to hold me up so that I wasn't sliding all over the car. Burying his face between my breasts, he kissed and sucked them greedily, pulling on my nipples with his teeth. He learned pretty quickly last night, playing with my tits was definitely the way to get me wet.

Pumping hard, he pushed inside of me dangerously deep, until I couldn't hold off any longer. Instead of crying out at the height of my orgasm, I bit down on his shoulder and raked my nails down his back. Growling, he gripped my hips hard and held me down onto him while he spilled every bit of him inside me.

Breathing hard, he pulled back and had the hugest grin on his face. "I have to say that was a first for me. I've never had sex with a girl *on* a car before."

"Me either. With a girl, I mean . . ." I giggled.

"Ooh. Now that's something I'd like to see," he teased. I smacked him and he pulled out of me so he could get my pants and tank top from the floor. Helping me off the car, he handed them to me and chuckled. "I'll tell you what. Why don't we do something today? No working out, no cars . . . just me and you. And tonight, we can eat dinner out on the beach again. Does that sound good?"

I slipped on my pants and tank top. "It sounds like heaven. Just as long as we can eat something fattening. A pizza would be good, followed by some Ben and Jerry's."

Smiling, he waltzed over to his tools and started putting them away. "I think I can live with that. Do you want to go in and take a shower before we go? There's a place on the pier that serves a killer breakfast. I can take you there."

Spending a day at the beach was going to be amazing. For the past couple of months, I'd devoted everything to working out and training for fights. I forgot what it felt like to actually enjoy life and the things around me. Paxton was helping me see all of that. Bouncing with excitement, I grinned and backed out of the garage. The day had just started and it'd already turned into the best one yet.

CHAPTER

II

Gabriella

BY THE TIME I got out of the shower and threw on some clothes, Paxton finally made it inside and rushed to get cleaned up. Since we were going to be out on the beach, I braided my hair down the side so it wouldn't get in my way with the California breeze. Looking around my room, I didn't know if I should pack up my clothes and move into Pax's, or if I should just wait. I only had a week left to spend with him before our deal was up. *I wonder what we'll do when our time is up . . .*

My phone ringing broke me out of my trance and when I looked down at it, I groaned. It was my agent, Garrett Wells. He wanted me to take the movie deal and I hated telling him I wasn't interested, but I couldn't bring myself to do it. Not to mention, I'd have to leave for filming and right now I didn't want to leave for weeks at a time. Was it because of Paxton? Maybe a little. Okay, so maybe a lot, but I wasn't going to tell Garrett that.

"Hey, Garrett," I answered.

"Why haven't you called me back?" he scolded. "I have so much shit to tell you, I don't even know where to begin."

"Try starting from the beginning."

"Ha-ha, very funny, Gabby. First, have you decided on accepting the movie offer? They really want you."

Biting my lip, I sat down on my bed and sighed. "Garrett, I know you want me to do it, but I don't think I'm ready for something of that size. I don't want to make a fool of myself if my acting sucks. I'd rather concentrate on my fighting career."

He huffed. "I had a feeling you'd say that. You're still young, so there are plenty of opportunities for you . . . which brings me to my next question. Allie Portman has asked to fight you. What do you say about that?"

Jumping to my feet, I gasped and started pacing the floor. *I can't believe this shit. This is huge.* Allie Portman was the current female Bantamweight champion. She was a force to be reckoned with in the ring. I'd never fought her, but I knew if I kept fighting there would come a time when I'd face her. About that time, Paxton walked out of his room and into mine, watching me with furrowed brows.

"Is this for a title fight?" I asked, biting my thumb nail.

"Yep, and she's ready to take you on. Do you think you'll be ready in two months with your brother taking time off? If so, I'm going to call and confirm."

"Yes," I shouted, running up to Paxton, smiling. "I'll be ready. Matt might be out of town but I have someone else who can help me."

Garrett sighed in relief. "Good, I was worried you wouldn't agree. All right, I'll get it scheduled. Next time when I call, you make sure to answer."

Bouncing on my feet, I was ready to get off and tell Paxton the good news. "I will. I'll talk to you soon."

After Garrett said his goodbye, I jumped into Paxton's arms and squealed. "Guess who's going to be fighting in two months for the title?"

He chuckled and swung me around. "Uh, I don't know. You, maybe?"

When he set me down, I couldn't stop smiling. "Yep, and you know what that means?" I asked, biting my lip.

"I'm assuming it means I've taken up coach duty?"

"That's right," I replied with a giggle. Allie was a hard hitter and I needed to train like a beast to get up to her speed and agility. I could do it, but it was going to be a lot of work.

Putting his arm around my shoulders, he led me out of my room and down the stairs. "If I do this, I'm going to need compensation. Hopefully, you don't expect me to work my ass off for nothing."

"And what exactly do you want?" I asked.

He paused and lowered his arm when we got to the door. "How about you stay here for the next two months until your fight? I don't have any scheduled right now, so I can devote my time to you. We can stay here and train in my garage and you can come and go as you please. I'll be your own personal trainer . . . in *all* things."

"How can I say no to that?"

He grabbed my hand and led me out the door. "You can't. Now let's go, I'm fucking famished. You made me work hard this morning."

Instead of going to his Hummer, he led us to his other garage and pressed a set of numbers in the keypad. I hadn't seen him go into that garage so I had no clue what was inside. When the doors lifted, he had two other vehicles in there, both different types of sports cars; one red and the other black. Then off in the corner he had a metallic blue sport bike, all shiny and pristine.

"Are you ready, sunshine?"

Paxton tossed me a helmet before rolling his bike out into the driveway. "You're kidding me, right?"

Chuckling, he slid his helmet down and fastened it, straddling the bike. The engine roared to life and my stomach rolled in knots. I had never been on a bike before and with the way Ryley and Camden rode, I was scared shitless to even want to.

Holding out his hand, Paxton beckoned me forward. "Come on, Gabby, it's not that bad. You'll have fun, I promise. Trust me."

"You and your damn promises," I grumbled, sliding the helmet on. "Just don't go too fast."

After he helped me fasten it, I straddled his bike and he guided my hands toward the tank. "Going fast is the best part. Just make sure you hang on to the tank." I wanted to hang onto him, but I guess safety was the number one thing. "All right, here we go."

Closing my eyes, I held onto the tank as hard as I could and squeezed my inner thighs against the bike when Paxton bolted us out of his driveway. My heart pounding in my ears was all I could hear, and of course, his laugh as he picked up speed. I was going to kill him.

After breakfast, Pax drove us around on his bike until my nerves were shot. I had fun, but every time a car would get near us I'd cringe. I could be fearless about getting into the ring and having someone come after me, but getting on a motorcycle was a whole other story. Paxton lived up to his promise because I did enjoy it . . . somewhat. He didn't do anything stupid, other than go fast, which meant I didn't have to kill him.

The rest of the day we spent together exploring Manhattan Beach. We walked up and down the boulevard and we even went to an aquarium at the end of the pier. I loved it. It wasn't only an aquarium, but a research facility as well. We stayed in there for hours while I talked to the various employees about their research results.

Now I was sitting on the beach out by Paxton's home, while he went to pick up a pizza from a local Italian restaurant. Beside me, I had a cooler packed full of goodies. The sun wasn't far from setting and I couldn't help but admire it.

Knowing Paxton would be back in a few minutes, I picked up my phone and dialed my brother. If he knew about my fight with Allie he would've called by now, so I assumed he didn't know. He answered on the third ring.

"What's up, Gabby?"

"A lot, actually. Have you talked to Garrett?"

"No, why?"

"Well, I thought I'd tell you that I have a fight in two months." Before he could say anything, I continued. "And no, you don't need to come home early from vacation. I got this."

"Yeah, but if you need me, I'll come. Who are you fighting?"

He was going to flip. "Allie Portman, for the title," I replied.

"Holy fucking shit, are you serious? I have to come home. You need me."

"No, I don't, Matt. Enjoy the time with Shelby and the baby."

"Let me call Mason. He'll be more than happy to help you while I'm gone."

I could hear the excitement and the conflict in his voice. He wanted to be there for me, but he also wanted to spend the time with his family. His whole life he spent trying to make sure I felt loved since our father left. I don't know what I'd do without him.

"Matt, that's not necessary. I have someone who's going to help me train."

"Who?" he asked.

Over my shoulder, I looked back at Paxton's house and saw him coming down the stairs of his back deck with the pizza in hand. "Paxton Emerson," I murmured.

"Paxton? How did that happen?" When I didn't reply, he sighed. "I guess I should've known. I saw the way you two acted around each other, but I never really thought anything of it."

"Why didn't you tell me he was the one who fixed your car?"

"I never thought about it. Besides, I didn't think it mattered. Are you two dating now?" He didn't say it with anger, so hopefully he wouldn't be pissed at me for being with a fighter.

"Actually, we are. I was afraid to tell you because of the whole thing with him being friends with Kyle. I felt like a turncoat."

Catching me off guard, he burst out laughing. "Gabby, no. Look, you can date whoever the hell you want. It took a while to get used to you making your own choices, but I trust you to make the right decisions. Paxton's not a bad guy."

"So, now you tell me," I grumbled. "I've treated him like shit for months because I thought he was part of Kyle's ploy to take you down."

"Serves you right for not being honest with me from the beginning." He chuckled. "Now on to the fight with Allie. If you feel like you can do this, then do it. Paxton's a good fighter and he might be able to show you things that I haven't. It's good to learn different styles."

"So you're not mad at me?"

"No," he laughed. "Just work your ass off until I get back in town."

"Will do. You don't have to worry about that."

After we said our goodbyes, it was like a huge weight had been lifted off my shoulders. For so long I was afraid of what my brother would think if he found out I had feelings for Paxton. Now I didn't have to worry about it.

"Please tell me you have some alcohol in that cooler," Paxton chided from behind. He sat down beside me and placed the box of pizza between us. It smelled heavenly. I hadn't had pizza in months.

"I have beer for you, wine for me, and two pints of ice cream for me as well."

Lifting the box lid, he pulled out a slice and took a bite. "I don't think so. There better be a peanut butter fudge one in there."

"There might be," I teased. Opening the cooler, I passed him a beer and pulled out my wine. "I talked to my brother." I poured the wine in a cup and took a sip, watching his eyes go wide.

"Did you tell him about us? About me helping you train?"

"Yes and yes."

"And?" he prodded. "What did he say?"

"He said there's no way in hell he's going to let you train me," I joked. "He said you sucked." I burst out laughing and then found myself tackled into the ground with my wine thrown into the air. "Hey, you made me spill my wine."

Guffawing, Paxton straddled my waist and held my arms down by my wrists. "Serves you right for saying some shit like that. What did he really say?"

"He said you were a good fighter and it might be beneficial for me to learn your style. Does that make you happy?"

Smirking, he leaned down, his lips achingly close to mine. "Did he really say that?"

I nodded. "Yes, and I also told him I was seeing you. He's not mad like I thought he would be. For years he's done everything possible to keep me away from fighters. And now he said it's my choice to make."

"And are you happy with your decision?"

Hooking a finger through his T-shirt, I pulled him

down closer. "More than happy," I whispered before pressing my lips to his. Letting my wrists go, he captured my face in his hands and kissed me slow and deep. I never would've thought that Paxton, a bad ass tattooed fighter with a record, would've ever had a soft side to him.

"You're so beautiful," he murmured, gazing down at me.

I kissed him again and spoke across his lips. "Thank you."

My phone rang, breaking the connection. Paxton sighed and helped me sit up. Why the hell did someone have to call at that exact moment? When I looked down, I had no clue who it was.

"Hello?" I answered.

"Gabby, it's Cliff."

Abruptly, I turned to Paxton. "Cliff, hi. What's going on?"

Paxton rolled his eyes and finished his slice of pizza. "Well, I just got home and found three flowers by your door. I thought I'd call and tell you. I haven't touched them and I haven't looked at the note. If you want me to, I will."

"No, that's okay," I said, packing up my wine. "I'm on my way." I hung up the phone and huffed. "I can't believe this shit."

"What's going on?"

Slamming the cooler shut, I sighed and looked into his concerned green gaze. "It looks like my visitor came again today. Do you mind going with me to check it out?"

He mumbled some explicit words under his breath and got to his feet. "This shit ends tonight, Gabby. I don't know what's going on, but whatever this person's doing, it needs to stop."

We both packed up our picnic and started for his house so we could drop it all off. "I agree," I murmured. "It's starting to piss me off."

CHAPTER 12

Gabriella

THE WHOLE WAY to my apartment was ridden in silence. Thankfully, Paxton opted to take the Hummer instead of his motorcycle. We were both on edge and the last thing I wanted was to be on a bike. When we got to my apartment, Cliff was leaning over the banister, waiting on us. He didn't seem too happy about seeing Paxton with me, but the feeling was obviously mutual when Paxton's gaze landed on him.

"Please try to be semi nice," I pleaded.

He scoffed. "We'll see."

At the top of the steps, Cliff met me there and gave a small smile. "I'm sorry I had to call and give you the news, but you told me to call if something happened."

"Thanks, Cliff. I appreciate it."

Paxton walked right on by us and went straight to the flowers and picked them up. I joined him. There were three black roses in his hand and all I wanted to do was step on them. This note, however, was a little more ominous than the others.

THREE . . .

YOU NEED TO
BE READY
FOR ME.

"What the hell? It gets weirder each fucking time," I hissed, snatching the note out of Paxton's hand.

"Are you sure this isn't your ex? I mean, come on, his best friend tried to screw over Ryley and Ash. It wouldn't surprise me if this asshole wasn't messed up in the head too."

"Bradley wouldn't do this. I know he wouldn't." Quickly, I turned to Cliff. "Did your friends find any fin-gerprints?"

He shook his head and handed me the other notes. "No. There was nothing other than mine and yours. I don't know what else they can do, other than patrol around to see if they can find someone lurking about. They have nothing to go on."

Sighing, I nodded and hung my head. "And I have no clue what I'm supposed to do. What if this person tries to attack me?"

"They aren't going to do that with me here," Cliff replied.

Paxton scoffed. "Well, first off, she's not going to be staying here anymore. She'll be with me. If this fucker wants to mess with her, they're going to have to go through me."

Cliff's gaze hardened. "If this person wants her bad enough, they'll get her. Just watch your back. It doesn't matter where she is." Then to me he said, "Be careful wherever you go. Don't trust anyone, especially strangers who try to talk to you." Turning on his heel, he trudged back to his door and glanced at me one more time before disappearing behind his door.

"I don't like this, Gabby. While you pack up your things I'm going to call Mason. He'll be able to tell us what we need to do."

Nodding, I opened my door and Paxton went in first, searching around to make sure everything was okay. When we were in the clear, I threw the notes on the counter and rushed to my bedroom. Load after load, I piled my clothes onto the bed. If I had to carry them all out in trash bags, I would.

I was going to be staying with Paxton for two months and I needed a lot more than what I originally packed. With everything going on, I was kind of glad I agreed to the two months. I sure as hell didn't want to be here.

CHAPTER 13

Paxton

WHEN I FIND out what sick fucker is leaving notes and flowers on Gabriella's doorstep, I'm going to cut off his goddamned testicles and make him wear them as a necklace. If she said it wasn't her ex I had to believe her, but dammit to hell, I wanted to find out who it was.

Gabriella was in her room packing so I stayed in her living room to make a phone call. Surely, Mason would know what to do.

"Hello?" he answered.

"Mason, it's Paxton. Do you have a few minutes?"

"Yeah, what's up?"

Over on Gabriella's kitchen counter, all three letters stared ominously at me. It took all I had not to rip them the fuck up and burn them. "I have a problem, or actually

Gabby does. Someone's been sending her black roses with notes on them. And they aren't exactly love letters."

"You've got to be fucking joking."

"I wish I was," I growled. "But I'm staring at it all now. I need to know what to do."

"How long has it been going on?" he asked. I could hear papers shuffling in the background. "I need to write all this down."

"For the past week she's gotten the flowers three different times. The first was with one black rose and a note and then so on."

"Can you take a picture and text it to me? I want to read the letters."

"Sure, give me a second." After lining the roses and the letters on the counter, I took a picture and texted it to him. "Okay, you should have it now."

The line went silent as I waited for him to look at the picture. The thought of knowing some psycho piece of shit was coming to her door made me furious. If she would've had her door unlocked, or even outside running her laps, there was nothing she could do to stop someone from harming her. What made it worse was that something could've happened to her this week, when I was waiting for her to come around.

"Paxton, you still there?"

"Yeah."

"All right, I'm going to get in touch with Ryan Griffin. He's the lead detective down in Vegas, but he'll know who to get in touch with. If things start getting really bad, I'll come down there myself; but for now, I'll fill him in on everything."

"What should we do? What do you think we're looking at here?"

Mason huffed out a frustrated breath. "I've seen shit like this all the time. With Gabriella being in the public eye, especially in the fighting world where she's surrounded by men, I'm surprised this hasn't happened before. She's a good looking girl and I know there are people who fantasize about that shit. There are some sick fucks out there."

"So, we're talking stalker here?"

"Pretty much. The only problem with this one is that the letters are very vague. I've seen instances where this sort of thing happened and we never see the girls again. It would be too late. This may turn out to be nothing, but it's not something we can play around with."

"What do we do in the meantime, while you get in touch with the other detective?"

"I want you to stay away from her apartment. Keep her somewhere where no one can get to her."

Thankfully, she'd been staying with me. I had a gate and plenty of guns in my safe. My uncle wasn't just big into racing, but hunting as well. I shot my first deer with him.

"She's been staying with me," I informed him.

He snorted. "Does Matt know?"

"He knows we're together, but not that she's living with me, or that she's being stalked by some psycho panty sniffer. She didn't want to worry him while he's on vacation."

"Fucking shit," Mason grumbled. "I just hope he doesn't call me because I don't know if I'll be able to keep my mouth shut. This could potentially be some serious shit we're dealing with."

I sighed. "I know. Let's just hope we get it figured out before it gets that far."

"Let's hope so," he agreed. "All right, let me get off and see what I can do. Keep me updated if anything else happens."

"Will do."

Mason hung up the phone and Gabriella waltzed out of her room with two trash bags full of clothes.

"You're staying for two months, not two years," I laughed, sliding my phone into my pocket.

"Two months is like two years." She dropped the bags onto the floor and caught her breath. "So what did Mason say?"

I picked up her bags and started for the door. "Basically, you have a stalker and I need to keep you safe until he figures something out."

"Do you think there's something to worry about?" she asked, concern etched in her voice. Gabriella was small, but she had a strong frame. I had no doubt she could fight her way out of most scenarios, but sometimes that just wasn't plausible.

"He said it'd be best for you to not be left alone. I kind of had that figured out already. He's going to get in touch with someone who'll be able to help us."

"I'm not going to be put on house arrest, Paxton," she remarked, crossing her arms over her chest. "This could go on for months and I refuse to let someone make me cower in the corner. I'm not going to lie, it freaks me out, but I can't be scared to go out in public."

If I had my way, she wouldn't go out at all. I'd be perfectly happy having her all to myself, twenty-four seven. "I'm not saying that, Gabby. God knows you're stubborn as fuck, and of course you're going to rebel, just to show this person that you aren't scared. We just need to be careful."

Huffing, she lifted one of the bags in her arms and started for the door. "And we *will* be careful. But, if someone comes after me, they're going to get the fight of their life."

"Let's just hope it doesn't come to that."

Once we were out the door, Gabriella locked it and we descended the three flights of stairs. Even though she tried to appear strong, I could see her gaze darting back and forth through the darkness. As long as she was with me, she'd be fine. There was nothing I wouldn't do to keep her safe.

CHAPTER 14

Gabriella

PAXTON WATCHED ME while I unpacked my clothes in the spare bedroom. My mind was a jumbled mess, thinking of who would be leaving me the messages. Every time, I came up blank.

"Are you okay?" he asked.

I folded up the last two shirts and put them away before joining him on the bed. "Yeah, I'm fine. It just sucks not knowing." I laid down beside him and placed my head on his chest, listening to the steady beat of his heart.

"You know I'm not going to let anything happen to you, right?"

"So what are you going to do, rescue me if something happens?" I teased lightly. "Like a super hero?"

"If need be," he answered in all seriousness. Shifting

his weight, he lifted up on his elbow. "I will do whatever I have to. If something happened to you, I'd spend every waking hour searching to find the answers. No matter what happens, I'll always come for you. I promise you this."

"You sure do make a lot of promises," I murmured. "It's got to be hard to keep up with them all."

"No," he replied, shaking his head. "Because the only ones I've made in my lifetime have been to you and Kacey. That's it."

Cupping my cheek with his hand, he leaned down and kissed me, gently opening my lips with his tongue. The smell of his skin and the taste of his lips were intoxicating. I never wanted to leave his arms. It was safe where I was. It felt like nothing could touch me while I was there. The feelings I had for the other men in my life didn't compare to the overpowering sense of fulfillment I had with Paxton. It was different, more complete.

Even though he drove me insane and made me want to pull my hair out, in the end, it was always a battle I was destined to lose. Our paths crossed and I believed that everything happened for a reason—that things were meant to fall into place when they did. I met him years ago, and didn't remember him because it wasn't our time. Now was our time.

Placing my finger to Paxton's lips, I broke our kiss and stared into his sea green eyes. We were both breathing hard and my heart was beating out of control. It was now or never. "Pax," I whispered softly.

He brushed the hair off of my face. "What is it, sunshine?"

Grabbing his hand, I held it to my cheek and closed my eyes. "I love you."

Silence fell over the room and it was as if time stood still. I waited for him to say it back, but he never did. Reluctantly, I opened my eyes and averted my gaze, hoping I could keep the tears at bay.

"Say it again," he commanded. "Only this time, keep your eyes open and look at me."

My pulse sped rapidly as I turned to stare at him. There was no rejection in his face, only raw, primal heat. It made me shiver. "I love you, Paxton. It took me forever to figure out what I was feeling, but there it is. I love you."

His fingers brushed the hem of my shirt and he slowly lifted it over my head, keeping his gaze on mine as he unclasped my bra. Gently, he cupped my breast and kneaded it with his warm, strong hands. Still, I waited for him to say something back, and he didn't. I could feel that he returned the sentiment, but I needed to hear the words. Instead, he lifted his shirt over his head and lowered his shorts. I helped him out and lowered my shorts as well.

Covering me with his body, he kissed his way up to my lips. "I want to make love to you."

My heart pounded. He pressed against my opening, but I reached down and took him in my hand, gliding it up and down before he could enter me. My thumb rubbed over the tip and a bead of moisture spread across my finger. I loved that I could turn him on.

"It feels so good when you touch me." He watched me play with him and his ass flexed as he pushed into my hand. Having had enough, he placed his hand on mine and moved it above my head, clasping his fingers through mine. The other he used to push a finger inside me and then another when I grew wetter.

The insides of my thighs were damp with need, ready

for him to take me, but he still worked me over with his long, lithe fingers. Pulling them out, he traced my nipples with my wetness and sucked them clean before placing his fingers in his mouth.

I moaned and bit my lip, resisting the urge to touch myself for relief. Thankfully, I didn't have to wait for long. Positioning himself at my entrance, he eased himself inside. Moaning, I gripped his hand and held it tight. With slow, gentle strokes he pushed in and pulled out, over and over. It wasn't hard and fast like when he'd fuck me. He was truly making love to me. No one had ever made love to me before.

When his lips found mine, I couldn't keep my eyes from blurring. Pax saw the first drop fall and his brows furrowed. "Gabby, what's wrong?" he asked gently.

I shook my head and squeezed his hand. "Nothing. Everything is right for once. Don't stop."

Picking his pace back up, he wiped away my tears and pressed his lips to mine. "Is it because I didn't tell you I love you? Because I do. I love you, Gabriella. I just thought I would show you first."

Lips trembling, more tears fell, but he kissed them away, licking them off of his lips. My heart soared. He loved me. Wrapping my legs around his waist, I lifted my hips so he could go deeper.

When my orgasm hit, his grunts of satisfaction and completion only made it that much more enjoyable. It was the most passionate and fulfilling level of intimacy I'd ever experienced.

Paxton unclasped his hand from mine and brushed the hair from my face. His green gaze bore into mine when he leaned down and placed his lips to mine. "I love you, Gabriella. I'm so in love with you it hurts. And don't even get me started on the lust."

I laughed through my tears and held his face in my hands. "I know the feeling."

CHAPTER 15

Gabriella

THE NEXT MORNING, I awoke in Paxton's arms. I didn't want to move for fear of waking him up, but his phone did it for me.

"What the fuck?" he muttered, his voice gruff from sleep. "Who the hell is calling so early?"

I looked over at the clock and laughed. It wasn't early . . . it was ten in the morning. When he looked at the phone, his voice softened. "Aunt Jackie?" he answered. I couldn't hear the conversation, but it sounded like something was wrong. "All right, I'll be there in a little bit. Just let me get up and moving." He stretched and got out of bed. "No, it's no problem at all."

"Everything okay?" I asked when he hung up.

Paxton chuckled and laid back down beside me, his

grin wide. "Oh yeah, it's nothing serious. My uncle's truck broke down, and apparently, he's trying to fix it. The last time he tried to work on a vehicle, he fucked it up beyond repair. I guess you can say I didn't learn my mechanic skills from him."

"How long do you think you'll be gone?"

He shrugged. "A couple of hours. Do you want to come with me? You might get a little bored."

Kicking the covers off, I stretched and arched my back, making my breasts perk up as they hit the air. Paxton growled deep in his chest. "Actually, I think I'll stay here and work out. But if you call me when you're on the way home, I'll be sure to be ready for you."

Grabbing a breast, he flicked his tongue over a nipple and bit down. My body jerked in response and I gasped. He circled his tongue around the bite marks and smirked up at me. "I look forward to it."

I moaned. "Go already, so you can get back."

Quickly kissing me on the lips, he jumped out of bed and disappeared into his room. A few short minutes later, he emerged wearing a pair of old, holey jeans and a faded red T-shirt. I liked that look on him. He was down to earth, unlike some of the other metrosexual guys I'd dated. Paxton could wear the old jeans and worn shirts and completely pull it off. That was who he truly was, and what killed me was that I had been so close to losing him because of my assumptions.

After the door shut downstairs, I heard his motorcycle roar to life and the sound faded off in the distance. My stomach growled, but I decided to rinse off in the shower before fixing something to eat. As soon as I dried off, I pulled out some running shorts and a sports bra and threw my hair up into a ponytail.

Now that Paxton was gone, I walked across the hall to his room and looked around. His walls were a dark gray and his large bed was covered in a similar shade of gray with silver bed sheets and black pillows. It was very masculine and modern.

On one of his dressers there were framed pictures lined with him in various times and places. There was one with him as a child, beaming at the camera with a man and woman on each side of him. Judging by the resemblance in appearances I'd have to say it was his parents. They looked so happy together. I didn't have any pictures like that.

Next, I recognized the picture with his aunt Jackie and who I assumed was his uncle Jack. And next to that was a group picture with Paxton and two other people. They were teenagers, but it didn't take much to recognize them as Kacey and Kyle Andrews. Kacey had her hair in braids with braces on her teeth and she was standing in the middle between Pax and Kyle. They all three looked so innocent with their beaming smiles, including Kyle. How he got to be so fucked up in the head was beyond me. People could change and thankfully Paxton figured that out before it was too late.

Not wanting to invade his privacy anymore, I made my way down the stairs and fixed a bowl of cereal and a cup of coffee. There was nothing exciting on the news, but I watched it while I ate. I never had much time to watch TV these days. When Ashleigh still lived with me I did, but that was because we loved watching our favorites. I couldn't exactly picture Paxton watching *Pitch Perfect* or the *Vampire Diaries*.

Once out to his garage, I turned on his stereo system and wasn't surprised to hear Avenged Sevenfold playing over the speakers. It was the same band he listened to every day he worked on his cars. The music was pretty good to exercise to as well.

I don't know how long I worked out for, but I was drenched in sweat and my muscles ached by the time I was done. Lying on the floor, I stared up at the ceiling to catch my breath but my heart sped back up when my phone rang. Hopefully, it was Paxton saying he was on his way back. If so, I needed to jump in the shower.

When I looked down at my phone, it wasn't him . . . it was Cliff. Dread overcame any sense of excitement I just had. "Hey," I answered. "Please tell me I don't have a new message waiting on me."

"I wish I could, but I can't."

Immediately, I jumped to my feet and started out of the garage. What the hell was this person doing?

"I know we don't really know each other, but I don't like this at all. I think you should go to the station. I'll follow you there if you want."

Then it hit me. I told Paxton I wouldn't go to my apartment without him. *Fuck!* "I can't come there right now, not without Paxton. I told him I wouldn't."

Cliff snorted. "Are you afraid I can't protect you? I think I'm insulted. If anything, I could kick *his* ass. Besides, it's daylight outside and there are people everywhere. I would be more worried at night, when people can hide."

Paxton was going to get pissed when he found out, but it was time I did something about it. "All right, I'll be there in about ten minutes."

"I'll wait by your door."

Cliff did as he said and was waiting on me by my door when I parked and glanced up. He waved as I got out of the car. Taking the stairs two at a time, I raced up them until I got to the top. He held the flowers out to me with a grim expression on his face. There were four flowers this time, all black with a note attached.

"Did you read it?" I asked, opening it up.

"I'm not going to lie, it's not good."

When I opened it up, my stomach twisted into agonizing knots. The message was the worst one of all.

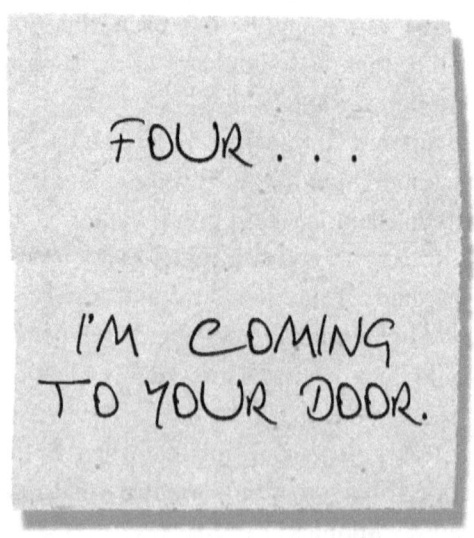

FOUR . . .

I'M COMING
TO YOUR DOOR.

"Holy fucking shit," I gasped, throwing the flowers down. "I need to get out of here."

Cliff nodded and picked up the flowers before guiding me toward the stairs. "Get in your car and you can follow me to the police station. We'll show them this and you can talk to them. Maybe they can help you figure out who it could be."

"Okay, let's do this," I said, keys in hand. I was ready to go and figure out what sick fuck was leaving cryptic messages by my doorstep. Cliff followed behind me as we started down the last flight of steps.

"I know I'm not on the squad yet, but I'll do whatever I can to help."

Over my shoulder, I glanced back at him and gave a small smile. "Thanks, Cliff. I really appreciate you doing this."

Before he could reply, his eyes went wide at something behind me. As soon as my foot hit the last step, a set of hands grabbed me by the shoulders and my head snapped to the front.

"And where do you think you're going?"

Holy shit, I was in some serious trouble.

CHAPTER 16

Gabriella

"SO IT WAS you leaving me those messages?" I ground out through clenched teeth.

Scar towered over me with his tall, bulky frame and dark eyes that almost looked black. He'd obviously acquired his name by how many he had on his body. Even across his shaved head on down to his cheeks there were scars. The only problem was, he wasn't alone. Two other men shadowed him and they didn't look like they were at my place for a picnic.

He snorted. "Hardly. Those are from Rage. Apparently, he's had a thing for you since that night you ventured into the Dark Side. You'll meet him soon, but for right now you have to deal with me."

"Gabriella, what's going on?" Cliff asked from behind.

Scar lifted a brow and smiled at me. "Yes, Gabriella, care to tell him what's going on?"

I knew damn well I couldn't say anything. I remembered the rules and I hadn't broken them yet. "Why are you here?" I growled. "I've kept my mouth shut and so has everyone else."

"That's true, but things have changed. I think we need to go upstairs and have a little discussion."

"And I think you need to get your hands off of her and back off," Cliff snapped. "She's not going anywhere without me."

Scar huffed and turned his dark eyes to Cliff. "Suit yourself. I hope you know what you're getting into."

If Scar was by himself I could probably jump over the banister and make a run for it. But with the other two goons, I wouldn't stand a chance. They were lean and lithe and obviously a lot faster. I didn't have a choice. Turning on my heel, I started up the stairs with Cliff by my side.

"Please stay out of this," I whispered. "You can't get involved with them."

"I don't fucking care. I'm not going to leave you alone."

"Dammit, Cliff, this is serious," I hissed.

It was obvious he wasn't going to listen, so I let him come with me to my apartment for fear he would call the cops. When I opened the door, Scar made me and Cliff go in first and then he followed with his goons. The tall one shut the door and stood in front of it, while the other started toward Cliff. They were both muscular, had shaved heads, and wore aviator sunglasses so dark I couldn't see their eyes. Neither one of them spoke either.

The shorter one with the shaved red hair and goatee reached for Cliff's arm but he jerked away. "Don't fucking touch me man."

"We're not going to do anything to Miss Reynolds, so calm the fuck down. We're just here to talk. Unfortunately, I can't have you listening in." Scar nodded toward Red and out of nowhere he clocked Cliff on the head with the butt of a gun.

"Oh my God," I cried as his limp body fell to the floor with a loud thud. Trying to rush to his side, Scar held me back with a hand on my arm.

"He'll be okay. Just a little headache when he wakes up. Now where were we?" He took a seat in one of my leather chairs and motioned toward the couch. "Please, have a seat."

"Gee, thanks," I grumbled. "I think I'll stand." I was in my own home and I couldn't even relax. I kept my eyes and ears vigilant and my body ready to fight. He said he wanted to talk, but I was in my apartment with three dangerous men, alone. Whatever happened, I wasn't going down without a fight.

Smirking, Scar sat back in the chair and crossed his leg at the knee, looking calm and relaxed. "I have a proposition for you, Miss Reynolds."

I snorted. "Yeah, I think I'll decline. You're what, ten years older than me?"

"So you don't like older men? It doesn't seem to bother you with Reaper."

"You don't know what you're talking about," I growled.

"Oh, don't I? I've heard you two have gotten awfully close. My partner doesn't seem to like it. He's been watching you."

"Who, Rage?" I asked incredulously. "Is he following me around? What kind of sick freak does that?"

"Obviously one that has a serious hard on for you. I suggest you calm it down with Reaper before something ugly happens."

"Is that a threat? Because let me tell you I don't do well with those. I think your partner needs to mind his own fucking business. What I do in my life is none of his concern."

"It is to him. And I wasn't threatening you. I'm warning you."

"Good, message received. Now get out," I thundered.

Scar tilted his head back and bellowed. "Damn, you are a stubborn little fighter, aren't you? But that's not all I'm here for. I have a *business* proposition for you."

"You've got to be smoking crack."

"Done that, didn't like it. Making money is my high these days."

"Then what?" I asked incredulously.

"Over the years, I've had different clientele come in with certain . . . proclivities. You've seen what goes on in the underground, so you can imagine how tastes change. Some like to fight with weapons and in Striker's case, he wanted to fight with glass."

Striker was Camden. The fights on that fateful night were highly disturbing. I'd never seen so much blood in my life. "If you're trying to get to a point, will you just get there already? You're confusing the hell out of me. I don't see where I can help you in this."

Scar got to his feet and walked around my living room, his eyes lit with excitement when he stared at me. "I want you to fight for me, Gabriella. Just three fights is all I ask. After having to pick up and leave Las Vegas, I need compensation. You and Reaper were the cause of that breach."

"We didn't breach anything. We've kept your secret and not said a word. I don't owe you anything."

"You might not, but Reaper does. I can always take this to him, but you don't want me to do that. I deal with men differently than I do women. Not to mention, Rage wants you, so we have to play this delicately. Reaper's a good fighter and I don't want to see him *ended* over this."

"Ended? Are you saying you're going to kill him if I don't help you?" He had to be bluffing. Surely, he wouldn't just kill someone for no reason.

In all seriousness, his dark gaze bore into mine and it didn't waver. There was nothing there, except a cold emptiness that made me shiver all the way down to my bones. He was dead fucking serious. Tears blurred my vision and I clenched my lips together hard to keep them from trembling.

"I have to do what I have to do, Miss Reynolds. I need your help and you're going to give it to me. If you don't, Reaper dies."

Bile rose to the back of my throat and I started to feel sick. I had no clue what I was about to agree to, but I had no choice. It was either agree, or Paxton died. Knowing there was no way to fight, I sat down on the couch and hung my head.

"What do I have to do?"

Gabriella

AS SOON AS Scar and his cronies left, I locked the door and rushed to Cliff's side. "Cliff," I murmured frantically. "Cliff, wake up." He took a nasty hit to the head but there wasn't much blood. *Thank God.* Quickly, I got a bag of ice and wrapped it up in a towel and placed it on his head. The coldness must've snapped him out of it because he winced and his lids fluttered open.

"So much for protecting you," he groaned low.

"It's okay. I don't think there's much you could've done against the three of them. How does your head feel?"

Slowly, he rolled over and tried to get to his feet. I helped him by holding onto his arm. "Who are they, Gabriella? What do they want with you?"

"I can't tell you. If I do, I'll be in even more shit. It'll be best if you leave this alone and forget it ever happened. The last thing I want is for something to happen to you just for being my friend."

"Are you going to tell Paxton?" he asked, narrowing his gaze.

Shaking my head, I put his arm around my shoulder so I could help him to the door. "I can't tell him either. This is something I have to do on my own. As soon as it's over, I'll be free."

"And what if you're not?"

"Then I'll have to figure something out."

There was a good chance I wouldn't be, but I couldn't tell him that. The whole deal with Rage had me worried. I had no clue who the douche nozzle was, other than he wanted me and I would meet him soon. The fact he was watching me didn't help matters.

What Scar asked me to do was degrading and completely against all of my morals. Not to mention, I was unsure if I could even pull it off. The proposition Scar asked of me not only required me to put on a show, but I had to be convincing, or Paxton's life was forfeit.

The worst part was, even if I completed his requests successfully, I still had another obstacle to overcome. *Rage.* He was going to come after me and I had no clue if I'd be ready. All I knew was that I had to be.

It all starts tomorrow.

After helping Cliff into his apartment and monitoring him to make sure he didn't have a concussion, he seemed to be doing fine. I recommended he go to the doctor, but he refused. It was only two in the afternoon and it felt like I'd gone through a week's worth of agony. Paxton still hadn't called, but I was already headed back to his house.

How was I going to keep everything a secret from him? During those three nights Scar needed me, I had no idea what I was going to tell Paxton. I couldn't just say, "Hey, I'm going out, see you later."

The thought of lying to him made me sick, but the thought of him dead was way worse. If he ever found out the truth, he was going to be so angry with me, even if it *was* to save him. I just hoped the flowers and the messages would stop.

The whole way to Paxton's house, I glanced in my rearview mirror at least a dozen times to see if anyone followed me. If Rage knew I was with Paxton, it made me wonder if he watched the house. I was happy Paxton had a gate around his property, but that didn't mean someone couldn't climb it.

I knew Pax could take care of himself, but for once I was truly scared for him. He wouldn't be on alert because he didn't know what was happening. What if Rage went after him? Whatever sick and twisted fascination Rage had with me, he better think twice about hurting Paxton. I protected the ones I loved, even if it meant putting myself in the crossfire.

Paxton called at the same time I pulled into his driveway. "Hey, you," I answered, trying my best to sound normal.

"I'm on my way home. It took longer than I thought."

"Did you get it fixed?"

He snorted. "What do you think? Of course, I did. He wants me to race tomorrow night. Do you want to come watch me?"

Ahh shit. "I can't," I said, sounding disappointed. "I talked to my mom today and she misses me. I felt bad because I haven't seen her in forever. She wants to do dinner and a movie tomorrow night."

"Oh," he commented. "I see. Well, there's always the next one, which is in two more days."

"And I'll be there." I had no clue if Scar needed me on that night, but I didn't give a shit. If he wanted me to keep this a secret from Paxton, he was going to have to work with me. "So, what do you want to do tonight?"

"I thought we could stay in. Maybe get in the pool? I can turn on the heat."

"Sounds good to me." In fact, it sounded more than good. If Rage was watching us, I was hoping it would be more difficult for him to see us if we stayed home. We'd be safe, for one night at least.

CHAPTER

18

Gabriella

THE WHOLE MORNING, Paxton spent working out with me and showing me new techniques with grappling. I loved to punch things and I was really good at jabs and combinations. My weakness was getting out of holds. Paxton was good at that, but unfortunately, we spent a lot of the morning trying to keep our hands off each other and dry humping on the mat.

After having some seriously hot sex in the shower, I stood under the falling water, letting it pound me on my back. I had two hours until I needed to be at my apartment. My nerves were shot, but I had to keep my wits about me if I was going to get through the night. Leaning my head against the wall, Paxton came up behind me and wrapped his arms around my waist.

"I don't think I can ever get enough of you," he murmured in my ear.

I hummed in agreement and turned to face him. "I know the feeling."

"What time will you be home tonight? Are you sure you don't want me to drop you off at your mom's?" He was worried about me going out alone, but yet, he didn't want to be overprotective to the point of smothering me.

If I weren't all wrapped up in a lie, I would've been happy to let him drop me off with my mom. "I'll be fine," I assured him. "It shouldn't be too late when we get done. I'll probably be here before you even get back from celebrating at the track."

"Well then, I'll see you tonight, sunshine." He tapped my chin with his finger and leaned down to kiss me. "I love you."

"I love you too," I whispered.

Setting me down, he washed off quickly and bolted out of the shower. "Wish me luck," he hollered, exiting the bathroom.

"Good luck." He wasn't the only one who needed it.

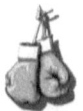

Once my gym bag was packed, I loaded up the Hummer and started on my way to the apartment. I had no clue who was going to pick me up, or where we were going, but I assumed I would be blindfolded. When I pulled up in the parking lot, I was about ten minutes early, and there was a car already waiting for me. It was a black truck with all black windows. I parked right beside it and looked over. The passenger side window rolled down and I looked in; it was the redhead who clocked Cliff over the head with the gun yesterday.

Groaning, I rolled down my window. "Let me guess, I have to get in the car with you?"

Smirking, he shrugged his shoulders. "You don't have to, but I would suggest you do. I don't like to see the boss pissed off and I don't think you would either."

Taking a deep breath, I let it out slowly and grabbed my bag. When I got into the truck I was expecting to see it full of other people, but it was just me and him. "Should I be insulted?" I looked around at the empty seats.

Red chuckled and held his hand out for my bag. I passed it to him for inspection. "You're just a woman," he explained. "I've seen you fight, but I'm pretty sure I can manhandle you into submission. Besides, you know what's at stake."

"And that's the only thing saving you right now," I mumbled angrily.

He tossed the bag in the back and passed me a blind-fold. "Put this on."

I did as he said and sat back in the seat. "What's going to happen when we get there?"

"Scar's going to go over everything with you and then we're going to put you in the cell so our bidders can take a look at you. If you do as he says, the night should be over pretty quickly and you can go back home."

"What if it doesn't?" I asked. "What happens to me if I don't win the fight?" Scar never went into detail on what would happen if I lost. He only told me what I was going

119

to be doing. There was a reason he wouldn't tell me be-
forehand. I was just hoping Red would tell me.

"I suggest you do whatever it takes to win, but I'm
going to let Scar be the one to give you details on what
happens if you lose."

Leaning my head against the seat, I took slow deep
breaths and cleared my mind. I needed to concentrate on
the task at hand. It was hard to do at the current moment.
Red kept quiet the rest of the way which suited me just
fine, and when the truck started to slow I knew we were
there.

"Keep the blindfold on until I take it off," he commanded. He got out of the truck and a few seconds later,
my door opened and he grabbed my arm, helping me out.
His hold was a little too tight, most likely because he
thought I would run away. There was traffic noise around,
but it was muted by the walls surrounding us. Feeling the
stuffiness of the air and the light draft on my skin, I'd
guess we were inside a vacant building, probably an industrial warehouse. However, there was a scent in the air that
I could definitely place; we were still by the coast.

Voices spoke around me, but I didn't concentrate on
them. I hated being blindfolded and I hated it when Paxton
made me wear one last time. It made me feel vulnerable
and weak, leaving everyone else the advantage. Another
few steps and Red guided me into a smaller room, shutting
the door behind us and releasing the blindfold. I had to
blink a few times to get used to the light, but when my vision cleared, Scar was sitting behind a desk with a smirk
on his face.

"Welcome, Miss Reynolds," he greeted. Red pointed
to the plush leather seat and I reluctantly sat, glaring at

them both. "Do you have any questions for me?"

"What ignorant jackass am I fighting, and can I cut off his dick?" I'd tried my best not to think about my opponent because Scar happily informed me yesterday that I wouldn't be fighting women, but men. Disgusting, vile men who want to manhandle women.

Scar bellowed so loud it hurt my ears. "You're one feisty little fighter. I like it. But no, you can't cut off their dicks, unless you can rip them off with your bare hands. There are going to be no weapons allowed in the ring. Remember, I need you to be scared. Let them push you around a bit. Make them think they have the upper hand. At the first sign of blood, it's over. They know this."

He slid a picture my way and tapped it with his finger. "This is who you'll be fighting tonight. He's thirty-eight years old and an obnoxious bastard. He owns a car dealership and thinks he's God's gift to women."

I looked at the picture and snorted in disgust. He was overweight with a beer gut the size of a watermelon. The guy could crush me if he got me down on the mat. "He looks disgusting," I spat, sliding the picture back. "Let me guess, he *thinks* he's God's gift to women, but can't get any and wants to take it out on some helpless female."

"Basically," Scar agreed. "He's slow as fuck, so your speed will help you out. All I ask is to make your struggle believable. One hit to that fucker's nose and you'll win. The people just want to see a helpless woman fight. They don't need to know who you really are."

"You're sick, you know that? How much are you getting off of this?"

His smile faded. "That's none of your business, little girl."

About that time, the door burst open and none other than Camden Jameson strolled in. His blond hair was a little longer than usual, and in messy spikes. From his side profile I could see the jagged scar going from his forehead down to his cheek. "Okay, so what exactly are you planning tonight? This douchebag out there says he's getting in the ring with a fucking woman. What retarded bitch would want to fight that jackass?" When his gaze caught mine, his eyes went wide. "You have got to be fucking kidding me."

"Striker, so nice of you to barge in," Scar muttered. "I brought in Gabriella to fight said jackass. She owes me."

"And you couldn't find another hard headed idiot to do the job? You do realize who her contacts are, don't you? If anyone gets wind of her being here, they'll come after you and everyone else here."

Scar sat back in his chair and clasped his hands under his chin. "I'm well aware of that, but she knows what's at stake. If she talks, then Reaper pays the price."

Camden scoffed and turned to me. "Since when do you care about Paxton?"

"Since they started fucking," Scar finished.

Rolling my eyes, I clenched my teeth to keep from saying something unintelligent. They could say whatever they wanted.

"Great," Camden snarled. "This is going to be one hell of a clusterfuck."

"Yeah, I'd say so, considering Rage wants her. He's none too pleased about this new development with Reaper."

"What does he have to do with this?" Camden narrowed his eyes.

This time, I spoke up. "I'd like to know the same thing. You never told me what happens to me if I lose a fight."

"Why, you go to Rage," Scar informed the room. "It was his idea to bring you in, so I let him make the rules."

"Hell no," Camden shouted, stepping forward. "You can't let her go to that psycho. I wouldn't send a whore his way, much less a woman of worth."

For Camden to come to my aid, meant my situation was beyond bad. Now I was completely and utterly terrified. Jumping to my feet, I felt sick to my stomach, but even more so, I was furious. "I didn't agree to be passed on to some lunatic, like a skank-ass whore. This is my life we're talking about. I agreed to help you recoup your money. I don't owe you anything else."

"I'm doing you a *favor*, Miss Reynolds," Scar retorted. "Rage wants you, but he knows the deal. In my house, he has to play by the rules. He's agreed to the terms. At least this way, you can escape from him. If you win, he lets you go. I can't promise he'll leave you alone once you're free, but for now you will be." He then turned his cold, heartless eyes to Camden. "And if you want to fight him for her, that's your deal; but if he doesn't agree to the fight, the rules still stand. She will go to him if she loses."

Clenching his jaw, Camden turned on his heel and slammed the door behind him. For once in my life, I wanted him to come back and tell me it would be okay. That had always been Ryley's job, but it looked like his brother was my only hope. I had no one else to turn to.

"What is he so upset about?" I demanded. "What's so bad about Rage, other than his name and the fact he's a psycho stalker?"

"I hope you never find out. I wouldn't have brought you here if I thought you would lose."

"Great, thanks for the vote of confidence," I muttered.

Scar smirked and then nodded at Red. "Take her to the room." Then to me, he said, "And while you're in there, try to make it look believable."

Red grabbed my arm and pulled me out the door. I had hoped Camden would be just outside, but he wasn't. I guess he wasn't going to help me after all.

CHAPTER 19

Gabriella

THE ROOM THEY put me in was different from the ones they had in Las Vegas. This time I could see and hear everyone who came past to make their bids. None of them could see my face though, as I was cowered in the corner with my head down. Little did they know I wasn't weak, or that I was seething inside. I hated them all. Their excitement over watching a man beat a woman was disgusting and depraved.

Over time, their murmurs faded and then disappeared. It wasn't long after that when Red opened the door.

"It's time to go," he said.

My thoughts strayed to Paxton. I hated not being there to watch him race, but if I didn't fight, he wouldn't be able to have any more of them. By the soulless look in

Scar's eyes, he contained very little humanity. It wouldn't surprise me if he'd killed at least a dozen men, maybe more. I knew he wouldn't have an issue going after Paxton. Getting to my feet, I kept my head down and trudged over to the door.

"Remember, I need you to be reluctant when I force you into the ring."

"Act like a scared little girl. Give the disgusting pigs what they want. Got it," I snapped. He stopped me by the door and I could hear the shouts of excitement on the other side. "What you people do is revolting. I'd like to see you get up in the ring with me."

"Is that a challenge?" he asked, his lip tilting up devilishly.

"Take it for what it's worth. I just know someone needs to teach you all a lesson." There was no way I could win against someone like him, but it sure would feel good to get one hit in. Stretching my arms overhead, I rolled my shoulders and snapped my neck to each side. I was ready to go. "Let's get this over with so I can go home."

"As you wish," he chuckled.

It was show time.

He grabbed both of my arms and I kicked and yelped as he threw the door open, dragging me inside. I'd left my hair down so it could cover the furiousness in my gaze. If looks could kill, everyone in the room would be dead. Through my hair I could see a row of women sitting in the 'victory' section by the ring. They were the women men had gambled with. What woman in her right mind would want to go to that fat, perverted bastard in the ring?

Red pushed me into the cage, making me fall to the mat. *Here we go.* Brushing the hair out of my face, I looked up in time to see the fat bastard heading my way, a dangerous gleam in his eyes. He grabbed a handful of my hair and lifted me to my feet, pulling me into him. It hurt like a bitch and I screamed when I could feel it tearing out of my scalp.

"You're a pretty little thing, aren't you? It's a shame I can't take you home with me." His breath smelled like stale coffee and eggs.

"Thank God for small favors," I hissed low. I wanted to vomit in his face, but he jerked me around by the hair, throwing me down on the mat. Scar was sitting by the ring, surrounded by other men, including Camden and another guy wearing a dark hood hung low over his face. It made me wonder if it was Rage under there.

All this fat fucker had to do was make me bleed and it would all be over. I was surprised my head wasn't bleeding, but thankfully, my hands came back clean. Before I could get to my feet, he grabbed my ankles and slid me to him, collapsing on my body. The breath whooshed out of my lungs and I gasped for air.

"Let's see here. How am I going to make you bleed?" His hard cock pressed into my thigh and in that moment, things were seriously getting fucked up, fast. There were plenty of ways he could make me bleed and I wasn't about to let him try any of them.

I wriggled underneath him and halfheartedly tried to fight him off. He laughed at my failed attempts, infuriating me more. What if I wasn't a fighter? What if I was really a helpless girl who was being used and abused like this?

His hand slid down to my breast and he squeezed, pushing it up to where it almost popped out of my shirt. "My wife never lets me bite her," he murmured, staring hypnotically at my skin. "Just thinking about sinking my teeth into your flesh is making me so fucking hard."

Eyes wide, there was no way in hell I was going to let him bite me. Licking his lips, he grabbed me by the shoulders, opening his mouth wide. Before he could strike, I looked over at Scar who nodded his head. Not like I was looking for his approval, but I was letting him know I wasn't going to take anymore.

My arms were restrained, but I still had my hands. It just so happened, I didn't have to play fair. I could be as dirty as I wanted and by God I was going to punish this fucker. Gripping his dick as hard as I could, I squeezed, twisted, and pulled until his body convulsed and he fell over, shouting in agony.

Quickly getting to my feet, I didn't waste any time before drawing the blood I needed to win. Swinging my leg up, I brought it straight down with punishing force, slamming my heel into his nose. Blood sprayed across the mat and the nasty bastard was done; I had knocked his ass out.

Sighing in relief, I fell to my knees and silently prayed to God, thankful I'd made it through the first fight. Two more to go, and Pax could keep his life.

I was taken to Scar's office and left there, when all I wanted to do was go back home and take a scalding hot shower. The door to the office opened and Scar strolled in with a wad of cash in his hands and a huge smile on his face

"I think this was a record night. You earned me close to a million dollars."

"Congratulations," I remarked dryly. "I'm ready to go home, can you get someone to take me back? I need to get there before questions are asked."

"Don't worry, you'll get home. Striker's offered to take you. I had several people request to fight you, but I'm going to stick to my word and leave it to two more fights. The longer you stay around, the greater the chance someone recognizes you. I can't have that."

"When do I fight next?" I asked.

"One week. I'm going to go through the requests and pick out which one will benefit me the most." He nodded toward the door. "Now go."

Without wasting another minute, I bolted out of the chair, straight for the door. Camden waited just outside, his arms crossed over his chest, blindfold in hand. He didn't even speak to me as I followed him down the hall to a set of doors. There we stopped and he put the blindfold over my eyes.

"I'm impressed," he murmured in my ear. "I feel sorry for Paxton if he pisses you off."

I didn't even respond as he led me to whatever car he was using. He helped me inside and shut the door. During that short time alone, I leaned my head back and peeked through the bottom of the blindfold. We were definitely in an industrial section of town. I didn't recognize it, but I did see a name on one of the buildings . . . *Tate Industries and Supply.*

When Camden got in the car, he started us on our

way. "You not going to talk to me?"

"I don't know what to say," I whispered. "How can you be a part of all this?"

"It's all I have."

"That's not true. You have me and everyone else. So what? You made a mistake and did something stupid. Okay, maybe something really stupid, but I know your brother still loves you."

"It's too late for that. I'm not the same person any-more."

"Oh, yeah, you're Striker now. The Camden I know and care about is still in there somewhere. If he wasn't, he wouldn't have cared if I was given to Rage."

He growled. "That's not going to happen. I could give a rat's ass if you fight tools like that jackass tonight, but handing you over to Rage is unimaginable."

The blindfold lifted and he tossed it in the backseat. We were in his sports car and on the highway headed back to my apartment. "Who is he Camden? What am I dealing with? He's left me messages with black roses all week. It's freaking me the fuck out."

His eyes went wide. "He's been doing that?"

"What does it mean?"

"I've never seen or talked to the guy because he walks around with a hood over his head, but I've heard stories. I don't know if any of them are true, but I'm not taking any chances where you are concerned."

So it *was* Rage with the hood over his head sitting with Scar and the others. "Tell me. I have to know what I'm dealing with here."

Sighing, he looked over at me and something passed in his expression. Concern? Fear? I couldn't tell. "He's killed people, Gabby. And not just anyone . . . they've all been women. I don't know how or why, but that's what I've heard."

The bile rose like a jagged knife in the back of my throat. Not only was this guy a stalker, but he was a murderer too. Tears stung the backs of my eyes. "What am I going to do?"

He pulled into the parking lot of my apartment and parked. "I don't know. Just be careful and don't tell anyone about this. They will go after Paxton if you do. And then nothing will stop Rage from coming after you." He nodded toward the Hummer. "Now get in and go straight to Paxton's. I'll follow you over there."

I opened the door and stopped. "Why do you even care what happens to me?" I asked, turning to face him. "You obviously didn't care what happened to your brother."

"Ryley and I are a completely different story. I've never had a problem with you."

He wouldn't face me head on and I knew it was because he wanted to keep his scarred cheek away. He was clearly ashamed of it. Was he possibly ashamed of what he'd done?

"You can always come back to us, Camden. You and Ryley can work this out. If I can see the good in you after what you did to my best friend, then that has to be something."

And just like that, he closed up on me, his gaze hard. "Don't call me Camden anymore. It's Striker. I'll do everything I can to keep you out of trouble, but after that, I'm done. Now go."

Camden had my bag in the back seat, so I grabbed it

and got out. Once I got into the Hummer, I found my phone and checked for messages. I had only been gone for four hours, which was perfect. That was enough time to make him think I ate dinner and went to a movie. I had to face Paxton and pretend everything was okay when everything was far from it. It would be my biggest acting role to date.

Luckily, when I got back to his house, he hadn't made it back yet. I had enough time to take a shower and crawl into his bed when I heard his car pull into the driveway. *Don't be nervous.* Paxton's footsteps sounded lightly on the stairs and when he opened the bedroom door the room illuminated from the hall light.

Quietly, he walked over to me and sat down, brushing a strand of hair off my face. "I know you're awake, sunshine. I can see your eyes fluttering."

A small smile splayed across my face. "I could be in REM sleep. Did you win?" I asked, opening my eyes.

He smirked. "Do you even have to ask? I kicked ass out there. Did you have fun with your mom?"

I answered while stretching and yawning, to help mask my lying. "Yes, we did. We're going to do it again next week."

"That's good," he murmured. "I'd do anything to be able to spend time with my parents again."

A tear escaped the corner of my eye and it fell onto the pillow. I hated lying to him. "Will you hold me?" I whispered.

Paxton stood and lifted his shirt over his head and climbed onto the bed. "Gabby, what's wrong?"

When he laid down beside me, I faced him so he could hold me tight against him. He smelled like exhaust from the race track, but I didn't care. I needed to be close to him, to feel safe. "Nothing's wrong," I assured him. "I just wanted you to hold me. I missed you."

Chuckling, he kissed the top of my head. "I missed you too, sunshine."

"Did you lock the door on your way in?"

"Yes, and I turned on the alarm. Are you scared someone's going to come here? You didn't get any more messages today, did you?"

"No, I just want to make sure the door is locked. You can never be too careful."

He held me tighter. "Trust me, I'm not going to let anything happen to you."

It wasn't just me I was worried about.

CHAPTER 20

Gabriella

THE PARKING LOT was packed when we pulled up and everyone waved at us as we drove past. The moment he got out of the car, his fans flocked to him and asked for pictures. Some people in the spotlight snubbed their noses at their fans, but Paxton didn't. He smiled and let them put their arms around him as he posed for picture after picture.

"You're actually good at this," I commended.

Grinning, he put his arm around me and turned me to face him. "Who would I be without them? Just some weirdo driving around fast in his backyard." Pressing his lips to mine, he held me close and didn't stop, even when people walked by and whistled.

"Get a room you two," a voice called out.

Paxton guffawed and let me go, keeping his arm

around my shoulders. The voice came from the blonde haired woman I saw hugging him the other night; his cousin, April. She had a smile on her face, holding the hand of a little boy, probably around six years old, with the same blond hair and blue eyes.

"So this is her?" she asked, smirking at Paxton.

"Yes, it is. She finally wants to be with me."

I smacked him on the arm and bumped him with my hip. "Hey, it was a hard decision with you acting all hot and cold, you big pain in the butt."

April held her hand out. "Yeah, well, that's Paxton for you. He'll do anything to get what he wants. It's nice to meet you."

"Same to you," I replied, shaking her hand. The little boy smiled shyly at me and moved behind her leg. "And who might you be?" I asked, bending down to his level.

April bent down and moved him forward. "Go ahead, tell her your name. Say, Adam."

His little voice was just above a whisper. "Adam."

He was the cutest little boy I'd ever seen. I didn't want to have kids any time soon, but I sure loved to talk to them. Ashleigh was going to have two kids in a few months and I was probably more excited about that than I was at my first fight.

"Well, Adam, it's nice to meet you. I'm Gabriella."

"Are you Uncle Pax's girlfriend?" he asked.

We hadn't exactly discussed it, but I assumed I was. I looked up at Pax, lifting my brows. "Do you have the answer to that one, Uncle Pax?"

Scooping Adam up into his arms, he chuckled and looked at me. "Sorry, little man, but the girl's taken. I tell you what though. Do you mind watching over her while I race? That way you can fight off all of the boys who try to kiss her."

"Do I get to kiss her?" he asked shyly.

Paxton smiled and winked over at me. "We'll see. She might let you give her a little kiss on the cheek. But now I've got to go." He held up his fist for a fist bump. "Give me some luck, tiger." Adam smacked his fist against Paxton's and giggled when he set him down. "All right, sunshine," he said, grabbing my hands, "I have to change and get ready."

Leaning up on my toes, I planted a kiss on his cheek. "Go get 'em."

He disappeared through the crowd and I was left alone with April and Adam. "Paxton tells me you're a fighter too. I never thought you'd be so beautiful," she said.

"Thanks," I laughed. "I'm new at it. My brother's been training me."

"Oh, I know your brother. I used to have the hugest crush on him a long time ago. I met him when Paxton was working on his car."

I think everyone had a crush on my brother at one time or another. "He did a good job on it. I didn't think anyone would be able to restore that piece of sh . . . I mean junk." Adam's little ears were listening and I didn't think April would want him hearing my foul mouth.

"Paxton's extremely talented. For the longest time, I thought we'd lost him when he started getting into trouble. He stopped racing and basically pushed everyone away. I'm glad to see he's matured."

I am too. Up ahead, I recognized Paxton's Aunt Jackie and pointed. "Isn't that your mother over there?" I asked.

April turned and smiled when she caught Jackie's attention. "Yep." She started off toward her mother and I followed. "She loves watching Pax race. So does my father, but my mom's always had a soft spot for him. He looks just like my aunt, Paxton's mother. My mom and she were really close. When she died, he was the only link to her."

"I can't imagine," I whispered. "I'm really close to my brother, and if anything happened to him, I'd be lost. My father left when I was three, so I didn't exactly have a close family bond."

April smiled down at Adam and then turned a weary gaze my way. "I know how you feel." As quietly as she could, she leaned over and whispered in my ear, "Adam's father left us when he was just a baby. It's been just me ever since."

"When I got older, I watched my mom struggle to make ends meet. I know it's not easy."

She snorted. "Tell me about it. I make decent money, but if it wasn't for Paxton and my parents, I'd be lost. Thankfully, now I don't have to work a night job anymore. Adam was bummed when his nights with Uncle Pax stopped."

Jackie closed the distance and scooped Adam up in her arms. "There's my big boy," she exclaimed. "What are you ladies talking about?"

April smiled and ruffled Adam's hair. "Oh, we're just talking about when I stopped working nights and Adam missed staying at uncle's place."

Jackie giggled and squeezed Adam harder. "Did you tell her about the time you picked Adam up at Paxton's and he was covered in tattoos? Apparently, he wanted to look like his uncle, so they went out and bought a bunch of temporary tats to put all over his body." Adam buried his head in Jackie's shoulder, smiling shyly.

"I bet that had to be interesting," I laughed.

With a huge smile on her face, April nodded. "Oh, believe me, it was. I took pictures of them together. They were both flexing their muscles in the mirror."

"You have got to let me see those pictures some time."

"Definitely. Come over and I'll show you one day."

"I'd be happy to."

About that time, Paxton came strolling out, dressed in his racing suit with a helmet tucked under an arm. He was walking alongside a man who I assumed was his uncle. He was a short man with perfectly combed white hair, dressed in a pair of greasy coveralls.

Looking over at us, Paxton grinned and nodded before turning to the stands and waving at the people. The crowd was insane, shouting and screaming from the stands. The energy was amazing, almost like it was in the arenas during a fight. Before getting into the car, Paxton walked over to me and presented me to his uncle.

"John, this is Gabriella. Gabby, this is my Uncle John."

"It's nice to meet you," I said, extending my hand.

John shook it and smiled wide. "Likewise, young lady. I've watched you fight. Good stuff."

"Thanks," I replied.

"Are you two staying for the party tonight? There's going to be fireworks."

Paxton lifted his brows, waiting on my answer. I nodded. "All right, then we'll stay, but I have a favor to ask," he said to his uncle.

"Sure, son, what is it?"

"Have you ever thought about having go kart races here? I know a pretty talented racer who'd love to tear up the track."

John pursed his lips and rubbed his chin. "Go karts, you say? Hmm . . . I never really thought about it. It could work though. I'm sure there are plenty of people out there who'd be interested in it. Who do you know that races?"

Paxton smirked and bumped me in the shoulder.

"You?" John asked, eyes wide. "I guess that shouldn't really surprise me. Give me a couple of weeks and I'll see what I can do. Surely, I'll find you some people to race against."

"That would be great," I exclaimed excitedly.

"Good, but right now, it's time to get this race started. Let's go, son."

Paxton kissed me quickly and jumped in his car before pulling off to the start line where the other racers lined up.

"He's up against some good racers tonight," John informed me. "One of them happens to be a NASCAR driver."

"Are you serious? Is that why there are so many people here?" The crowd had doubled from the other night. I never paid attention to NASCAR, so I had no clue who it was.

"Yep. His name is Derek Anderson. I've been trying to get him to come out for months."

The engines revved, drawing my attention to the track. "Which car is he in?"

John pointed to the bright yellow sports car beside Pax. "He's in that one. I took a look under the hood . . ." He whistled. "That car is one hell of a beast. I hope Paxton can take it."

I had no doubt. The red light overhead slowly made its way down the line to the yellow, and once it flipped to the green, they were off. Tires squealed and smoke blew across the field, obscuring my view and bringing the smell of exhaust and burnt tires through the air. Once it all cleared, Paxton and Derek were neck and neck, battling it out.

One lap down and they were sticking together. "How many laps do they have to do tonight?"

"Since Derek's out there, we upped this race to ten. It's the most Paxton's ever raced. I hope he can keep his wits about him."

Judging by the way he drove, he looked perfectly all right. However, once they headed into the fourth lap, Derek got the lead and pulled in front about a car's length ahead. *Come on, baby.*

I wished he could hear me cheering him on, but there was no way anyone could hear with the deafening sounds of the cars zipping by. The fifth and sixth lap came and went with Paxton trailing closely behind. The other drivers had all fallen back, and barring any accident or mistake, they were out of the race.

When they started in on the tenth lap, everything changed. Out of nowhere, Paxton picked up speed and gained some ground. Slowly but surely, he moved up inch by inch, until he was even with Derek again. The race was almost over, but he needed that push to drive him over the finish line first.

Folding my hands together, I closed my eyes and prayed. *Please, let him win.* As soon as I opened my eyes, his car lurched forward and he bounded past the finish line in first place. The crowd went crazy and so did I, jumping up and down, screaming. When Paxton pulled up into the pit, he raced out of his car and threw off his helmet before scooping me up into his arms.

"You were so fucking hot out there," I shouted excitedly. "You did great."

"Are you my prize for the night?"

"Do you want me to be?" I challenged.

"You're damn right, I do. And I can't wait to unwrap my gift." Setting me down, he smacked my ass and was met with April and Jackie, who threw their arms around him. I stood back with John while his fans rallied, congratulating him.

"That's Derek," John noted, pointing to the tall redhead approaching Paxton. He had a huge smile on his face. At least he wasn't disgruntled about losing. Paxton shook his hand and they talked for a minute before Derek retreated, giving Paxton his space.

The crowd began clearing out of the stands, with some coming down to the field, and others leaving the premises. Once the stands were empty, Paxton said goodbye to his fans and took my hand.

"Come on," he ordered. Dragging me away from the crowd, he led me up the stairs to the announcer's box. It was dark in the room, but when Paxton opened the door, I realized it was just tinted windows.

"Why isn't there anyone in here?" I asked, sticking my head in. It was dark, but there was illumination from the switchboard lights.

"John only has announcers for the professional races. That's usually on Saturday nights."

"Ah, I see. You're normally in the ring on those nights."

Putting his hand on the small of my back, he gently pushed me inside. "I love fighting more than anything, so I'd never turn down a fight to come here."

"What are we doing in here?" I turned around and Paxton was locking the door.

"I want my prize and I want it now. What do you think about that?"

Running my finger along the desk, I licked my lips and smiled. "Then come here."

"You don't have to tell me twice."

Roughly, I reached for the waistband of his jeans and ripped them open, freeing him. I pushed him toward the desk and got down on my knees. The tip of his dick glistened and I flicked my tongue across his wetness. He jerked in response and I smiled.

Closing my lips around his length, I took him in as far as I could go and sucked hard. His fingers knotted in my hair and he held on as I tortured him with my tongue. Yanking his pants down to his calves, I brought one hand up to aid my mouth and used the other to lightly pull on his sac.

"Fuck," he growled. "Ah, *shit* that feels good."

After a few more pulls on his cock, I stood up. "I can't wait any more." As I unbuttoned my jeans and pulled them down to my thighs, he turned me around and pushed me over the desk. With my pants and underwear just below my ass, my legs were held tight together.

Dipping two fingers into my center, he pulled them

out and spread my juices around, making my entrance slick. Leaning over me, he pressed me into the table. His mouth trailed down the side of my neck and then he bit my shoulder.

"What if someone comes looking for us?" I moaned.

"Then they'll just have to wait until I'm done." With one nudge from his cock, he found his prize and slammed home, groaning from the extra tightness. Our bodies slapped together and the desk wobbled as he pummeled into me, taking me as hard as he could. Standing up, he grabbed my ass and used it to pull me harder onto him.

I knew he was close by the sound of his moans and grunts. I couldn't hold off any longer. My body clenched, and my stomach and legs shook as I exploded, milking him. After a few more pumps and a smack to my ass, Pax came hard, jerking above me.

Making a satisfied noise, he kissed my back and then slowly pulled out. There was a roll of paper towels on the back counter so he grabbed them and helped clean me up before wiping himself off. Every day he amazed me more and more. I'd never known anyone as selfless as him.

Unfortunately, I knew there were also bad sides of him that I didn't know about yet. There were things he wouldn't talk about, especially from the times of his troubled past; when he was friends with Kyle. Did it even matter? No, because whatever he did in his past was just that, his past.

Standing up and turning around, I whispered softly, "I love you."

Holding my chin, he leaned down and pressed his lips to mine. "I love you too."

We pulled our pants back up, and while we were buttoning them, my thoughts became too loud and I had to address them. "I have a question."

He glanced over at me, brows furrowed. "What is it?"

"Are you ever going to talk about what you did? Like when you fought at the Dark Side?"

Sighing, he tilted his head back, averting his gaze. "Gabby, it's not something I like to talk about. One day I'll tell you, but we've come so far and I don't want you seeing me differently. I'm not like that anymore."

"I know you're not," I murmured wholeheartedly. "I just want you to know that you can talk to me about things." I just wished I could tell him about what was going on, to warn him.

He put his arm around me and led me to the door. "And I appreciate that, sunshine. Now why don't we go out there," he said, pointing to the field, "and have us some fun."

He opened the door and we started down the stairs. "So what did Derek talk to you about? Your uncle said he was a professional racer?"

"Oh yeah," he replied excitedly. "He wants to race with me one night next week."

"Wow," I exclaimed. "Look at you go. I bet that'll be fun." Hopefully, it'll be on the night of my last fight. Walking down to the field, we were almost out of the stands when I reached into my back pocket. My phone wasn't there. "Uh-oh, I think my phone fell out of my jeans. I'll be right back."

Starting up the stairs, he called to me, "Do you want me to come with you?"

"No, that's okay. It'll only take a second." The door wasn't locked, so I went right in and found my phone on the floor. Every time I looked at it, I cringed, thinking there was going to be a text from Scar. Thankfully, there wasn't any.

When I got out the door, Paxton was down below talking to Derek again. They both peered up at me and I smiled. However, that smile didn't last long when something out of the corner of my eye caught my attention. My spine tingled and the hair on my neck stood on end. There was danger around and I could feel it. On the ground, staring ominously back at me was a single, black rose . . . crushed, the petals disfigured and torn.

CHAPTER 21

Gabriella

THE NIGHT WENT by in a blur, but I had to pretend everything was okay. Left and right, I looked over my shoulder, sensing his presence like the fucking plague. He was there watching me and I had no clue who he was. I was glad when Paxton wanted to leave.

As soon as we got back to his house and he was in the shower, I checked the doors and the alarm a gazillion times to make sure everything was good. I didn't like feeling watched and I sure as hell didn't like someone stalking me.

It was now morning and I'd watched the sun come up, with Paxton sleeping beside me. He'd held me in his arms, but even as I had laid there, I was scared.

"How many cups of coffee have you had?"

The coffee machine finished spitting out the last of my pumpkin spice and I took a sip. "Three, but who's counting?"

"How can you be so tired? You look like you haven't slept a wink. You're not getting sick are you?"

I yawned and took another gulp. "Your mouth is moving and all I'm hearing is that I look like a pile of shit."

Paxton chuckled and finished up our eggs and bacon. He'd wanted to make breakfast, so I happily let him. "No, you don't look like shit. You just look like you're about to pass out, even after drinking all of that damn caffeine. Do I need to take it easy on you today?"

"No, I need the training. But maybe I can take a nap this afternoon?"

He passed me a full plate and a bottle of water. "I'll think about it. After you finish eating, meet me in the gym. I'm going to go ahead and get started."

After a couple bites of eggs, he slipped a piece of bacon into his mouth and headed out the door. I was half tempted to crawl back upstairs and lay down, but I couldn't slack now. I needed the training and my title fight with Allie was the most important one of all. Once my food was gone, I rushed upstairs, brushed my teeth, and washed my face. My poor eyes were puffy and I looked pale. I was never pale.

My phone went off. Quickly, I dried my face and rushed to pick it up. It was Camden. "What do you want?" I answered.

"Damn, look who woke up on the wrong side of the bed this morning."

"I'm not in the mood, *Striker*. Apparently, Rage followed me to the track last night and left a calling card. I haven't slept at all."

"Are you serious? That dude really has some fucking problems."

"Yeah, I'd say so. Now, what do you want? Paxton's going to be looking for me if I don't get out there to him."

"Are you two living together?"

"For the time being. I sure as hell don't want to stay at my apartment by myself right now," I snapped.

"Calm down, Gabby. I told you, I'm not going to let Rage get to you. Listen, Scar wants you to come in tonight. He's moving next week's fight up. I'll be at your apartment at seven. Oh, and make sure to wear something a little more sexy."

"What?" I spat. "I can't come tonight. What am I supposed to tell Paxton? He's going to start getting suspicious."

Camden sighed. "Just tell him you're going out with some friends. It's not that fucking difficult. You don't answer to him."

"I know that, asswipe. Maybe one day, when you get into an actual relationship, you'll understand. He's worried about me with this whole stalker deal."

"I told you, I'm not going to let him get to you, not while I'm there."

I scoffed. "Forgive me, if I don't have much faith in you right now. I haven't forgotten what you did to Ashleigh and your brother. For all I know you could be in on all of this."

The line went silent, but then he came back on, his voice hard. "You're right, I could be, but I guess you'll just have to trust me. Besides, you have no choice. Don't make me have to come hunt you down because that's exactly what Scar will do if you don't show."

I didn't have a choice. "I'll be there," I said, then hung up. I didn't want to hear anymore. Regrettably, there was someone else I needed to call. When I dialed his number, he answered almost immediately.

"Hey," he answered.

"Hey, Mason. I have a problem."

"You mean, bigger than what you had yesterday?"

"Much," I replied sadly. "Camden called and he's picking me up tonight. Apparently, I'm scheduled to fight."

"I thought it wasn't for another five days?" he growled.

"The plan changed. But there's something else that happened last night. While Pax and I were at the race track, we kind of slipped away for some alone time and when we were done I found a demolished black rose outside the door. What am I going to do?"

"Gabby?" Paxton called.

"Fuck," I hissed. "Paxton's coming. I have to go."

"Dammit, this doesn't give me enough time. I'm not going to know where you are."

Then it hit me. Quickly, I rushed into the bathroom and shut the door. "They blindfolded me while I was there, but I did see the name Tate Industries and Supply on a building nearby. We were also by the coast. I could smell the salt in the air."

"All right, I'll look it up. Just play it safe tonight and win the fucking fight."

Even if I didn't truly believe it, I said, "I'll be fine. I have to go." I hung up and turned the phone off. Paxton's footsteps raced up the stairs and then he was in the room.

"Gabby, you okay?"

Turning on the water, I washed my hands and opened the door. Paxton was shirtless, his skin sweaty from working out. "Yeah, I'm fine," I told him.

He leaned against the doorframe, narrowing his gaze. "Are you sure?"

I dried my hands on the towel hanging on the rack and laughed. Hopefully, I wasn't being paranoid. "Yeah, why wouldn't I be? Are *you* okay?"

He stepped out of the way so I could pass. "Actually, that's why I came in to get you. Derek called and said he wanted to race tonight."

Breathing a sigh of relief, I plastered a smile on my face. If he went, it would save me from having to lie. "That's great. You're going to go, right?"

Nonchalantly, he shrugged. "I want to, but I want to make sure you're okay about it."

"Please, I'm perfectly fine," I said, rolling my eyes. "You'll have fun. But right now, let's get my ass in shape. I want you to show me how to fight in a real situation, like my life depended on it." We started down the hall toward the stairs.

"Why are you asking that?"

If I was going to be fighting dirty, I wanted to know how to do it, especially if I needed it to defend myself. When I didn't answer, he stopped and turned me around by my shoulders.

"Is there something you're not telling me?" he asked.

I almost reached up and tucked the hair behind my ears, but refrained. "No," I lied. "I just want to make sure I'm prepared, you know, in case something ever happened to me. I know how to fight, but that's not going to cut it if someone really wanted to hurt me. I figured with your experience, you'd have a few tricks up your sleeve."

Chuckling, he put his arm around my shoulders and led me outside. "I swear, your brother is going to kick my ass when he finds out I've corrupted you."

No, he'll thank you for saving me.

CHAPTER 22

Gabriella

BEFORE PAXTON LEFT, I kind of hinted that he should maybe go out for drinks after he and Derek were done racing. I needed to make sure I had plenty of time to get back before he did. Luckily, he'd showed me some moves that could possibly help me out. One was how to gouge someone's eyes out. I prayed I wouldn't have to ever do it, but if it came down to me or my attacker . . . I'd sure as fuck do it in a heartbeat.

I packed my 'sexy' clothes in a gym bag because there was no way in hell I was going to wear it out. Scar was just going to have to settle with seeing me in a pair of yoga pants and a T-shirt for the time being. Once Paxton pulled out of the driveway in his blue race car, I sat by the window and watched the gate close. Thankfully, it wasn't dark out yet, but it was going to be soon. There was something about night that made things more menacing. It was always the time when the evil came out to play. I think that was why I never liked Halloween much.

The time was closing in on seven o'clock so I hopped into Paxton's Hummer and headed on the way to my apartment. When I got there, Camden hadn't arrived. Making sure the doors were locked, I sat there and waited, scrolling through my phone at the latest news.

Someone banged on the car window making me yelp. "What the . . ." Clasping my chest, I blew out a nervous breath and waited for my heart to calm. It was Cliff. I rolled down my window and huffed, "You scared the shit out of me. What are you doing?"

"I was going to ask you the same thing," he said, leaning on the window. "I thought you weren't supposed to come out here alone?"

Camden chose that time to pull up on the right side of my car, gesturing for me to get in.

Furrowing his brows, Cliff gaped at him before settling back on me. "Who the hell is that now? You're not in trouble again, are you?"

Grabbing my bag, I shook my head and put my hand on the handle. He stepped back so I could roll up the window and open the door. "No trouble here."

"For some reason, I don't believe you. I didn't get hit over the head for no reason the other day."

"Cliff, just leave it alone," I warned. By now, Camden had gotten out of his car and circled around the Hummer.

"Gabby, let's go."

Cliff stepped protectively in front of me. "She's not

going anywhere without me."

Camden snorted, reaching for my bag and I let him take it. "Gabby, do you want to handle that for me? If I do, it's not going to be all peaches and cream."

"You can't come with me, Cliff," I said, walking past him. "There are rules and you've already been in the cross-fire because of me."

"I don't care." Grabbing my arm, he turned me around. "I can get you out of here, if you just say the word. Something's wrong, I can feel it."

I wish I could tell him, but it would only endanger him more, including myself. "Please, just drop it," I hissed low. "I have to go with him. I don't have a choice."

Gritting his teeth, he let me go and I got in the car with Camden. He pulled us out of the parking lot and passed me a blindfold. "You know the drill, babe."

Rolling my eyes, I put it on and sat back in the seat. If memory served me correctly, we had about thirty minutes until we would reach our destination. "I assume you don't have any guns or weapons in your bag?" he asked.

"No, but I wish I did. Maybe I could put the worthless fuck I'm about to fight out of his misery quicker."

Camden chuckled. "I have no doubt you'll do that to-night. Scar's picking men he knows you'll beat."

"So are you trying to say I should thank him for not handing me over to Rage?" I snapped.

"He just wants his money and if you beat these men, he gets it."

"I can't imagine the kind of trouble I could get into doing this shit. I'd be kicked out of the UFC for sure."

"Let's just hope that doesn't happen," he said. A few seconds passed but then his voice dipped low. "You've got to be kidding me."

"What?"

"It looks like your friend decided to follow us."

This can't be happening. "What are we going to do?"

The sound of Camden's phone beeped as he dialed out a number. When I heard the sound of a voice on the other end, I could tell it was Scar. "We have a problem," Camden growled. "Apparently, we have a tail. Some dude who's friends with Gabby." After more words were spoken, Camden hung up and sighed.

"What's going on?"

"It looks like your friend just bit off more than he can chew. He fucked up, Gabby. If he gets in, I don't know if he's going to make it out."

"He's just trying to protect me, Camden. I can't let anything happen to him."

"There's nothing you can do. As soon as we get inside the gates, it's all out of our hands."

After the thirty minutes were up, the car came to a stop and Camden helped me out. My heart lurched with guilt, especially when I heard Cliff's voice in the distance. It disappeared all too quickly.

Camden pulled me along. "I really hope you brought something else to wear besides those fucking yoga pants."

"Yes," I spat. "I was afraid Scar would make me fight naked if I didn't."

"Several guys *have* requested it, but Rage was the one who got you out of it." We got inside and he pulled the blindfold off. "He doesn't want the others looking at you."

Or having sex with me. He made that abundantly clear when he left a disfigured rose outside of the announcer's box. The guy was seriously insane, delusional. I had no words. Scar's office was just down the hall, but when I looked behind me there was no sign of Cliff. I could only pray he was okay. The door to Scar's office was open and inside he sat at his desk, waiting on me.

"So we meet again," he said with a wolfish grin on his face.

"Not by choice," I grumbled.

"And it seems you brought a problem with you this time. Now, how am I going to handle this?" Pursing his lips, he gaped at me, tapping a finger to his lips.

"I'll take responsibility for him," I blurted out. Camden pinched me in the side and I hissed. He obviously didn't like that decision.

"Are you sure you want to do that?" Scar asked.

"Yes."

"All right, it's his life on the line if you lose. I hope you're prepared for that." Lowering his gaze, he busied himself with the stack of papers in front of him.

"So you're going to kill him if I lose?" I gasped.

Scar didn't even acknowledge me. He just waved his hand in the air dismissively. "Take her away, Striker."

Gripping my arm, Camden dragged me out of the office and down the hall. "Camden, *stop*. If I lose, you can't let Scar kill him," I cried.

"There's nothing I can do. It's just the way things are here." He opened the door to one of the cells and pushed me in. "Change clothes and I'll be back to get you soon."

I was so angry and terrified, my body shook. Cliff's life was in danger and his fate rested in my hands. Tonight, there was no playing the innocent female. If I had to win the fight, I was sure as hell going to do it *my* way.

CHAPTER 23

Gabriella

WHEN CAMDEN CAME back to get me, his eyes went wide when he took me in. I ripped up my yoga pants and T-shirt so that it would give me the movement I needed, but still the amount of skin exposure Scar wanted. My hands were wrapped and I was in full warrior mode. No smile, no sign of weakness, just me and the task at hand. I was going to make my opponent suffer.

"Gabby?"

I had thought Camden was going to help me; that maybe there was a heart inside of him somewhere. Unfortunately, he was just like the rest of them—a murderous, money hungry, piece of shit. For one night, I was going to give in and let my anger fly. I would show them all, including Rage, what *my* rage looked like.

"Sorry, Striker, Gabby's not here right now. If Scar wants a fight, he's going to get it. And if Rage wants a helpless female, he's going to see I'm not that girl. I'll fight him and everyone else who tries to fuck with me and Paxton."

Camden stepped out of the way so I could pass. "I need to tell you something."

I stopped in front of him, but kept my gaze toward the end of the hall. "I don't want to hear shit from you," I sneered. "I don't need your help or anyone else's. All of you can go to hell."

Camden jerked me out into the hallway and pinned me against the wall. I yelped as the breath whooshed out of my lungs and his fingers grasped my chin tight, tilting my face up. "I may be a monster in your eyes, Gabby, but there's something you need to know. I was walking by Scar's office and I heard him talking to someone. I don't know who, but I think it was Rage." Letting my chin go, his eyes darted up and down the hall and then he leaned closer. My gut clenched.

"They want to go after Paxton," he said. "It's been their plan all along. Rage wants to fight him and kill him. That way he'll get to you." Camden put his hand over my mouth when I gasped and put a finger to his lips. "Be quiet," he hissed.

When I nodded, he removed his hand. "How do they plan on getting him here?" I had the sinking suspicion I knew.

He sighed. "By the look in your eyes, I think you already know. They're going to use you as bait. I'm telling you this because I need you to be prepared. Paxton needs to know. You have to tell him what's going on."

This whole time, I thought I was saving Paxton. How could I be so stupid? "When are they planning on doing this?" I asked.

He shrugged. "I'm not sure. You guys just need to be ready. But right now, it's your turn to fight." Grasping my arm, he led me down to the end of the hallway and opened the door. The energy pouring off of the crowd around the ring made me gag. It was thick with the stench of malevolence and sex. I wanted them all to suffer.

"We'll be ready," I murmured low. "Have no mistake about that."

The man in the ring was dressed in a suit for Christ's sake, and pacing around the ring. *He must be trying to fulfill his fantasies of being Mr. Fifty Shades.* He had a flogger in his hand and everything. The thought of him using that on me, or anyone, made me sick. I wasn't the type of girl to like that stuff. If two people wanted it, that was one thing; but with him using it on me for torture, it just pissed me the fuck off.

With his hand on my arm, Camden led me through the crowd, but I jerked out of his hold. "I don't need help to get into the ring," I hissed low. "I'm more than happy to get in there by myself."

Still, he kept his pace beside me. "Focus, Gabby. You're pissed, I get that. Don't let your anger blind you. Just kick his ass and be done."

"Don't worry, I know exactly how I'm going to make him bleed." And I was going to make him bleed a lot.

I stormed up the steps and into the ring, which made the man falter. I wasn't the weak and scared little girl he wanted. Camden shut the cage door and locked it so neither one of us could get out unless he opened it. That didn't bother me. The man circled around the ring and snapped the flogger against the mat.

"Do you like the sound of that? It's going to sound great once it hits your flesh."

I countered him, concentrating on his movements. "Or better yet," I began, "the sound of *your* screams when I'm done with you, you worthless piece of shit."

Snarling, his arm reared back, but I jumped out of the way and tumbled across the mat before the flogger could touch me. One hit with it and it would tear my skin wide open. If I bled, I was in trouble.

His eyes went wide when I deflected him. "You stupid cunt. Do you honestly think you're going to get away from me?"

He charged again and I kicked his legs out from under him, making him topple to the ground. The flogger flew out of his hand and I jumped for it, grabbing it before he could. His hand grasped my ankle and he pulled me down to the mat, but that was as far as he would get with me. I kicked him in the face so hard, blood instantly gushed out of his nose. It wasn't enough though. The fight was considered over, but I didn't want it to be over.

Camden opened the door and waved for me to come out, but I shook my head. With the flogger in hand, I clenched it tight and glared at Scar and Rage, the man who I assumed was hiding underneath the hood. Maybe he was so fucking ugly no one could stand to see his face. "You want blood?" I shouted to the crowd. "You want to see women suffer? How about I show you what happens when you mess with the wrong one?"

Lifting the flogger in the air, I slapped it down on the guy's back and the ripping sound of his clothes and skin echoed through the room. Blood seeped through his shirt and I smiled. The laugh that came from within sounded so foreign to my ears that I barely recognized myself. I was so overwrought with anger, I wanted to make everyone suffer.

The man crawling across the floor tried to get away from me, but I kept smacking the flogger against his back. All I could see was red, I didn't want to stop. I blocked out everyone and everything except the man on the mat who passed out cold, most likely from the pain. His back was covered in blood and his shirt was in tatters. Before I could hit him again, a set of arms grabbed me around my waist and jerked me out of the cage.

"I'm not done," I shouted angrily. As I was being pulled away from the cage, the men surrounding it gave me a wide berth. Fear was all I could see in their faces and I relished in it. The flogger was torn out of my hands and when I looked down they were covered in blood. My body started to shake and my teeth chattered. There was so much blood.

"Gabby, you're *shaking*," Camden shouted. He lifted me up in his arms and rushed me out of the room. The lights above started to blur and I couldn't stop shivering. I felt like I wasn't even in my body anymore. My chest rose and fell as I struggled to breathe and I could hear my heart pounding in my ears.

"She's going into shock. Get me something to wrap her up in," Camden demanded. He set me on the couch in Scar's office and rushed out of the room. The last thing I remembered before the blackness took me was a cloaked figure leaning over my body and the feel of his hands on my face. I was frozen as he touched my body and wrapped me in a blanket. Even when he leaned over and kissed me, I couldn't move.

"Soon," he whispered. "Soon, you'll be mine." My eyes closed and I surrendered to the darkness. I was never going to be his.

CHAPTER 24

Paxton

AFTER DEREK AND I practiced around the track, he showed me some techniques to help maneuver the turns easier. I also showed his crew some of the ways to make his car faster and more efficient. It was a win-win. We were on our second round of drinks when a call came through on my phone.

"Hey, sunshine," I answered.

"Sorry to disappoint."

"Who the fuck is this?" I growled, getting to my feet.

"Pax, it's Camden. Calm the fuck down. Where are you? I need you to get back to your house right now."

"Why do you have Gabby's phone? Where is she?" I demanded.

"She's with me, but I don't know how to unlock your

gate. Either you give me the code or I wait on you."

Pulling out my wallet, I set a wad of cash onto the bar. Derek and his guys watched on in concern. "I have to go," I told them. "Something's wrong and I have to get back." Derek nodded and I didn't waste any more time. Rushing out to my car, it roared to life, the tires screeching as I stormed out of the parking lot.

"Why can't she unlock the gate?" I asked. I didn't trust Camden and I sure as hell wasn't going to give him the code.

"Look, just hurry the fuck up and get here. She needs help." And with that, he hung up and left me hanging. I had ten minutes to get back to my house and it was the longest ten minutes of my fucking life. So many questions raced through my mind. Why the fuck was she with Camden? And why couldn't she talk to me?

When my house came into view, Camden's car was parked outside the gate. I bolted out of my car and rushed up to his. Covered in sweat, he rolled his window down and the heat blasted out. Gabriella was in the passenger seat, draped in a blanket and passed out. Not only was she unconscious, but she was covered in blood.

"What the fuck happened to her?" I shouted, running to her side of the car. Ripping the door open, I reached in and took her face in my hands.

Camden sighed. "It's not her blood, Pax. We need to get her inside now."

My body shook with rage. I wanted to kill him for whatever he did to her. Storming over to my keypad, I punched in the code and the gates slowly opened. Once Camden started in through the gate, I got back into my car and followed.

I carried her inside, taking the steps two at a time, and laid her down on my bed. Camden came in and went straight to my bathroom and turned on the shower. The steam started billowing out into my room.

"What happened?" I demanded, clenching my teeth.

"I'll tell you in a minute, but we need to get her in the hot water. She's covered in blood and she's in shock."

He tried to take the blanket off of her, but I pushed him out of the way. "Don't you fucking touch her. If it wasn't for her, you'd be dead right now."

"Yeah, well, take a fucking number."

Once I had Gabriella out of the blanket, her clothes were torn and she was covered in dried up blood. I carried her into the bathroom and slammed the door so I could undress her. Holding her naked body in my arms, I sat her on my lap in the shower and let the hot water beat down her skin. The blood washed away, turning the water a light red as it washed down the drain. She had it everywhere, even underneath her nails.

Taking the soap, I washed every square inch of her skin and hair. Thankfully, she started to come around and gasped when her eyes opened. She tried to fight me, but I held her harder.

"Sunshine, it's me," I murmured. "You're safe now."

After she was rinsed off and clean, I held her in my arms and wrapped her up in a couple of towels.

"Pax?" she whispered.

"Yes, I'm here." Now that she was covered, I took her into my room where Camden still sat waiting.

"Is she okay?" he asked.

I walked right past him and pulled the covers away on my bed and laid her down, covering her back up. Her skin was cold, even after the hot shower, so I rushed to my closet and snatched some extra blankets. Once she was secured underneath, her breathing started to calm and she passed out again.

"You need to start talking, now," I demanded angrily.

After having a chance to get a good look at Camden, I saw even he was covered in spatters of blood. I hadn't seen him in a while, but I'd heard about the jagged scar he now harbored on his face. Running his hands through his hair, he went to the corner of my room and sat down in the brown leather chair.

"She's been fighting for Scar," he blurted out.

Eyes wide, I jumped off the bed, my fists clenched by my side. "What the fuck do you mean she's been fighting for Scar? How's that possible? She's been with me." Not to mention, I thought Scar was in Vegas.

"She's only done it twice, and I assume she had to lie to you to get away."

Gabriella wouldn't lie to me. She'd been with me every single day since she moved in. Then it hit me . . . the date with her mom. And then again tonight, when I was with Derek and his crew. *Motherfucker.* No wonder why she'd been acting weird. "What is Scar doing out here?"

"After my fight with Ryley, he moved everything out to L.A. He knew from the beginning that he wanted to get here and blackmail Gabriella."

"What happened to her? Start from the beginning and tell me everything."

Camden sighed and hung his head back. "She did it for you. Scar threatened your life unless she did as he said. So, she did it. She agreed to three fights and after that you'd be set free. But as you could probably guess, that's not the truth. The letters she's been getting are coming from a guy named Rage. Do you know him? It looks like he's had a fascination of her after seeing her the night of the fight in Vegas. He's the one who wants you out of the way."

So that was who it was. I'd heard of Rage, but I didn't know the details. He wasn't around when I fought at the Dark Side. I heard he was ruthless, and never hesitated to kill. But if he was there with Gabby . . .

"So help me God, he better not have touched her," I stormed. "Has he done anything to her?"

Camden looked at me and shook his head. "No, not yet. After she almost killed a guy tonight, I got her out of there as fast as I could. When I told her they were coming after you, she snapped."

"A guy? What was she doing fighting a guy?"

"That's the twisted part," he explained. "Scar wanted to cater to his clientele and give them a weak girl they could fuck around with. He made a lot of money off of her. After tonight, I don't know what's going to happen. She did her own thing and dominated the douchebag. The pussy even pissed himself because he was scared."

Over my shoulder, Gabriella laid quietly in my bed. She asked me earlier to show her some moves on how to fight dirty. That was the reason why she asked, she needed my help. "So what happens now? You say they're coming after me . . . when?"

"I don't know," Camden answered truthfully. "But I do know they're going to use Gabriella as bait. They'll take her and make you fight."

"Then I'll fight. I'll do anything for her."

Getting to his feet, Camden glanced over at Gabriella,

eyes melancholy. "I sure hope so. I've never met Rage, but I do know he's one fucked up bastard. There's no telling what he'll do to her if he wins."

That was not my worry, because now that I knew, I would be ready. I would fight until the end. Even if I had to kill him.

CHAPTER

25

Gabriella

PAXTON WAS IN the ring with the hooded Rage and the sound of swords clanging together hung in the air. I screamed, but no one could hear me. Rage sliced Paxton's midsection, and I raced up to the cage, fighting to get in. Over and over, I pounded on the cage, my own fists broken and bloody from the metal.

Lying on the ground, Paxton turned his tormented gaze toward me. "I'm sorry," he whispered before the life left his eyes.

Rage's face was covered by the hood, but he dropped his sword and started for the cage door. It swung open and he came straight to me. I tried to run away, but I couldn't move. Arms holding me firm, I fought against him, beating against his chest. Lifting his arm, he grasped the top of his hood and slowly started to pull it back. I was scared to see what was underneath and fought even harder.

Tears blurred my vision because Pax was dead. He was gone. "Get your hands off me," I screamed.

"You belong to me now, Gabriella. I'm not letting you go."

"No!"

"Gabby, wake up." I heard the words in Paxton's voice, and it made me cry harder. "Open your eyes," he ordered again.

The pillow was soaked when I opened my eyes. Looking around, I found Pax in front of me, alive and regarding me wearily.

"You're alive," I whispered.

It'd been just a nightmare, but then I realized I was still in it. My mind was a jumbled mess, and I had no idea how I'd gotten back to the land of the living. The last thing I remembered was falling into darkness with Rage above me saying I'd be his soon. By the look in Paxton's eyes, he knew what had happened, that I had lied to him.

"You know?" I asked.

He nodded. "Yes. Camden brought you home, covered in blood and in shock. Why didn't you tell me what was going on?"

My eyes burned. "Because I didn't want you involved. I knew you would try to come to my rescue. They would kill you."

"It looks like Rage wants that anyway, Gabby. I don't think we have a choice. I just hate you had to go through all of this alone."

"I'll be fine. It was terrifying, but I got through it. The

fighting wasn't a big deal. It's the knowing that Rage was there, watching me. He was there at the race too, Paxton. He's been following us."

His eyes went wide. "What do you mean he was at the race? How do you know that?"

My head hurt, but I sat up and held the blanket to my chest, clutching it tight. Just knowing a homicidal stalker was just outside the room as we had sex made me shiver. "It was after our go in the announcer's box. When I went back up there to find my phone, I saw a black rose near the door, all broken and torn apart. He was there."

"Goddammit," he hissed. "Has he followed us everywhere?"

I nodded. "Scar told me Rage was angry and didn't like seeing us together. I think that's why he moved the fights up the way he did. Rage is getting impatient."

Paxton got to his feet and ran his hands through his hair. He was shirtless, wearing only a pair of boxers. "We need to figure out what to do. They're going to come for you."

Then Mason came to mind. He was going to help and now that Paxton knew what was going on, we could all work together. "I know that, but I have a plan. I haven't told anyone, not even Camden about this."

Paxton came back to the bed and sat down beside me. "What is it?"

I reached for his hand and brought it to my face. My dream still felt real, but in all reality, there *was* going to be a fight and it wasn't going to be good. "I've been talking to Mason," I explained. "He's going to get a team put together like he did in Vegas, when he busted the last underground fighting ring."

"I can't believe you've done all of this behind my back." He didn't sound angry, but his jaw was firm, his green gaze unreadable.

"I wanted to protect you," I whispered.

Lifting a hand to my face, he brushed his thumb across my lips. "You don't have to protect me, Gabby. I just wish you would've confided in me. We could have figured this out together. I'm not going to let Rage or any other fucker take you away from me."

"You promise?" I asked.

Slowly pulling the covers back, he stood and dropped his boxers to the floor, covering me with his body. He spread my legs with his knee and leaned on his elbows, his mouth close to mine. I opened for him and moaned when he went deep, tasting me greedily.

"I promise, Gabriella. Whatever I have to do to keep you safe, I'll do it. Even if it means killing this guy to keep him away from you. I promise to always be there for you and trust you no matter what. You just have to trust me too."

"I do," I whispered.

It was early morning and we were both awake, lying in each other's arms in silence. We hadn't let go of each other since we'd made love. Thoughts of the night before still plagued my mind. I had no clue what happened to Cliff, and I had no idea what happened to the guy I fought.

If Camden hadn't stopped me, I probably would've killed him.

"I think I almost killed someone last night," I confessed. "And what's worse, I don't know what happened to Cliff. He could be dead right now."

"Cliff? What does he have to do with all of this?"

Here we go. I licked my dry lips and explained, "When Camden came to get me last night, Cliff saw us out in the parking lot. He knew there was something off with the situation and his cop instinct kicked in, so he followed us. I don't know if Scar did anything to him. When I got up to go to the bathroom, I tried calling and texting, but nothing yet."

Paxton held me tighter, his body my safe haven. "Whatever happens, there's nothing you can do, Gabby. I hate to say it like that, but he shouldn't have followed, especially when you told him to stay out of it. That was stupid on his part."

A tear escaped the corner of my eye. "I know, but I still care about what happens to him."

His jaw tensed. "Well, maybe he'll call today. Now tell me about the fights."

"The first fight wasn't so bad. I pretended to be scared, which really pissed me off because all I wanted to do was beat the shit out of the fat fuck. He pulled my hair and dragged me around the mat. I had the worst headache after that. When he got me down on the mat and I felt how hard he was over it, I can't begin to tell you how sick that made me."

"How did you get up?"

Clearing my throat, I could still remember the way it felt to have his hard cock in my hand as I pulled it as hard as I could. The pain had to be excruciating, but he deserved it. Hopefully, he wouldn't be able to have sex for a very long time.

"Let's just say I broke his junk, if that's even possible. Imagine a laffy taffy machine pulling taffy this way and that."

"Holy fuck," Paxton growled. The tension and anger flowed off his body in thick waves. "I can't believe you had to do that. Where was Camden in all of this?"

"There wasn't anything he could do. He already threatened to fight Rage for me, but if he kept pushing, he'd get booted out. If he wasn't there, I don't think I'd have handled it as well."

Paxton sighed. "I know, but I'm so goddamned furious at him right now. To be a part of something like that is unforgiveable."

"You used to be," I whispered.

"Not like that. I would never have approved of them making women fight men. I was the one who fought fuckers like Rage, the ones who liked to torment women and children."

Turning in his arms, I looked at him. "What are you talking about?"

"That's what I did when I fought in the underground. I took on worthless cocksuckers who liked to rape women and children. There were men who would come in and brag about that shit all the goddamned time."

Tears blurred my vision. "Oh my God. That's horrible."

"Needless to say, I challenged them. I didn't even need weapons to fuck them up. I was angry to the point I snapped each and every time. There was no holding back."

I reached up to touch his cheeks but he averted his gaze. He knew what I was about to ask. "Did you kill them?" I asked softly. There was no judgment or accusation in my tone. If he killed them, I wouldn't think differently of him. Because deep down, I wanted to kill the guy I fought last night. People that liked to hurt, kill, and rape innocent people shouldn't be allowed to live.

"Paxton?"

"Honestly, I don't know. After the fights were over, the men were taken away. I never knew their names, so I wouldn't even know if they showed up on the news. But let's face it, they didn't give me the name Reaper for no reason."

"Paxton, look at me, please," I begged. Reluctantly, he lifted his gaze and clenched his jaw. Now I knew why he didn't want to talk about his past. It pained him to think about it. "I'm not going to judge you. I love you. If it makes you feel any better, I wanted to kill the fucker I had to fight last night. I probably would have if Camden didn't pull me away."

Resting his forehead to mine, Paxton breathed me in. "When I saw you covered in blood, I can't begin to tell you how terrified I was. I didn't know what was going on."

"I'm sorry you had to see me that way. I was so angry and disgusted with what I had to do. I just snapped seeing all of those men who got hard up over watching a man attack a woman. He wanted to flog me, so I turned the flogger on him."

Paxton huffed. "And even now it's not over. We need to call Mason and tell him everything that happened." He kissed me on the lips and then slid out of bed. "I think I know of someone else who can help, but I need you to be okay with it."

"Who?" I asked curiously.

Sliding on his boxers, he pulled a pair of shorts out of his drawer and put them on. "He's someone you don't like very much. In fact, no one likes him right now, but he might be the key we need."

"Who?" I repeated.

Once he had his shirt on and headed for the door, he sighed and turned around to face me. "Kyle," he admitted hesitantly. "He owes it to us to help."

"What makes you think he's going to?"

"I don't know, but it's worth a try. I'm sure he knows who Rage is and if he does it'll help us. I have to try."

Even though I didn't want that cocksucker helping us, I nodded. "Okay, I trust you. I'll call Mason, while you deal with fuckhead."

As soon as he disappeared down the hall, I laid back in bed and closed my eyes. It felt like a war was coming and I was right in the middle of it. But then thinking of war made me think of Cliff. *Oh my God, I don't know if he's okay.* When I left last night, I was out of it.

My phone was on Paxton's dresser so I bolted out of bed and fumbled with the keys. They shook so bad I could barely dial. Once his number was punched in, I waited for him to answer. When he didn't, I called again . . . and again. He never picked up.

"Fuck, this can't be happening," I cried. This time I texted him.

Me: Call me back ASAP!
Me: I have to know you're ok!

Please let him be okay.

CHAPTER 26

Paxton

I HADN'T TALKED to Kyle since everything went down with Kacey. All I knew was, he could barely walk and was in a wheelchair. The fucker got what he deserved. I didn't want Gabriella to hear our conversation so I headed out to my garage. He most likely wasn't going to answer the phone, but I had to try anyway. After I dialed, it rang about four times. I was about to hang up when his voice came over the line.

"What the fuck do you want?" he snapped. "To rub it in my face how I fucked up and everyone hates me?"

Typical Kyle. "Leave it to you to think it's all about you. I'm not calling to rub anything in your face."

"Then why are you?"

"How are you?" I asked. He used to be one of my

closest friends, and I could only imagine how it must feel to be helpless.

He scoffed. "Like you care. I'm stuck in a fucking wheelchair, how would you feel?"

"Have you talked to Kacey?"

Kyle huffed, but then his voice turned weary, defeated. "No, she won't talk to me. Not that I can blame her. I'd do anything to have her forgive me. I didn't know Liam was going to do what he did." He paused. "Have *you* talked to her?"

"No, I've been a little preoccupied with some things. I have some questions for you though."

"Ah, so you need something from me."

"Yes, and I'm hoping you'll help me. Do you know a guy named Rage? I heard of him a long time ago, but I never met him." The line went silent. "Kyle?"

"I know him. I'm just wondering why you have an interest in him."

"Who is he?" I asked. "What's his name?"

"Like I'm going to tell you that. The dude's fucked up in the head. If word gets out that I told you, my crippled ass will be dead in an alley somewhere."

"It's better than Gabriella turning up dead," I thundered. "But I guess I'm not surprised you don't want to help."

"Wait, what does Gabriella have to do with this? Please tell me he's not stalking her." When I didn't answer, he knew the truth. "Fuck me," he stormed. "What has he done?"

"Let's see, he wants to kill me and he's been sending her black roses and cryptic messages. Not to mention he's been following her."

"Goddammit. You need to keep her away from him. The guy's been on the run for years. From what I've heard, he raped and stabbed a woman because she cheated on him and then turned around and mutilated the guy before killing him too. It's fucked up."

"And now he's after me and Gabby. Please, Kyle, I need to know his name. I have to know what I'm up against." And to see what all we can find out about him. We had no clue what he looked like and if Gabriella didn't know, then he could be anywhere.

"Are you going to fight him?" he asked.

"Yes. He's going to challenge me. I have to make sure he can't ever go after Gabby."

Kyle sighed. "Permanently?"

"If that's the only way to make sure she's safe, I have no issues ending him. He's no worse than the other men I've fought."

"You were always so noble weren't you? Always wanting to fight the bad guys."

"Please, just give me his name."

The line went silent and each second that passed I wanted to rip out his throat. I shouldn't have to beg to get a fucking name, especially when that person wanted to kill me and do God only knew what to Gabriella.

I was about to hang up and just say fuck him when his voice came back over the line. "All right, I'll give you his name. This guy fights dirty, Emerson. You need to be on your guard at all times."

"I will," I promised.

"His name is Josh Davenport. That's all I know about him. I'd seen him around the Dark Side at times, but never actually spoke to him. He kept to himself."

Sighing in relief, I headed back inside so I could give Gabriella his name. She would need it to give to Mason. "Thanks, Kyle. You probably just saved our lives."

He sounded different on the phone, almost like he was lonely, needy. I shouldn't feel sorry for the guy because he got what he deserved, but with his willingness to cooperate I couldn't help but be grateful. After I hung up the phone, I rushed inside to Gabriella who paced my bedroom floor, holding her phone in her hand. She had one of my T-shirts on tied at the waist with a pair of leggings and her midnight hair pulled high into a ponytail.

Last night, she experienced what it was like to turn to the darkness. It had changed her and I could see it in the determination in her eyes. They were going to pay, and I was going to see it through.

"Have you talked to Mason?" I asked.

"Only briefly. He said he was going to call me right back. I'm just waiting on him. So what did fuckface say?" She hated Kyle and probably always would. Hell, I wanted to hate him, but if the information he gave us was solid, then I'd be indebted to him.

"He gave us a name," I informed her.

"And you believe him?"

I shrugged my shoulders and approached her. "I don't know, but it's worth a shot."

From the look on her face, she didn't have much faith as she paced my bedroom floor. Her phone buzzed, and she took a deep breath and let it out. "It's Mason. Here we go."

Now, all we had to do was wait and see what we had to do next.

CHAPTER 27

Gabriella

"SO YOU'RE SAYING this guy's name is Josh Davenport?" Mason asked. He was already in L.A., but laying low like he suggested we do until he got all of the facts.

"Yes, that's the name Kyle gave Pax."

Mason scoffed. "I can't believe he called that fucker. If he's screwing with us, I'm going to make sure he can't walk for the rest of his goddamned life."

"Paxton thinks he's really trying to help us and I have to trust him. As much as I hated turning to Kyle for help, I think it was the right move."

Mason already knew the timeline and every single thing that'd happened over the course of the last two weeks. His team was all prepped and ready to go at a moment's notice. So, if Paxton had to fight tonight, they'd be ready. That gave me some sense of relief.

"All right, Gabby, I'm going to study this timeline and I'll call you back sometime this afternoon. I dropped off the trackers with Carter early this morning. You and Paxton need to go by there and pick them up as soon as you can."

"We will. Thank you, Mason."

"Don't thank me yet. This isn't over. There's still a lot that could go wrong." Mason was a realist, but I was an optimist. I had to believe everything would be okay. Good always triumphed over evil, right? Or at least that was how I saw the world.

Once we hung up the phone, I sat down beside Paxton. "We need to run by Carter's. Mason left us some trackers there, so he and his team can follow us."

Getting to his feet, he pulled me up by my hand and put his arms around my waist. I relaxed into him and laid my head on his chest. "I swear I never thought being with you was going to be so difficult," he teased.

"Hey," I exclaimed, playfully trying to push him away. He held on tight and wouldn't let me go. I didn't want him to let me go. "I can't help it if some deranged lunatic is obsessed with me. You are more than welcome to walk away. I'll fight Rage all by myself."

Letting me go, Paxton took my face in his hands. "I'm not going anywhere, Gabby. As long as you want me, I'll be here." He smiled and kissed me, before leaning his forehead to mine.

"Then I guess you're not going anywhere."

"Except to the gym," he said, pulling me out of his room. "We need to get to Carter's and get those trackers. We have to be ready. I'm not taking any chances where you're concerned."

As soon as we got outside, the tension rose. I never knew when we were being watched, but we both kept vigilant. I tried to keep the weight of impending doom from pressing me down, but it was overwhelming. There was something brewing and I knew it was going to happen soon.

When we got to Carter's, we stayed and worked out like we would on any other day. Apparently, Carter was told to put the package inside my gym bag because after we were done, I saw it inside. Everything was supposed to be normal and we pretended it was.

"What's in it?" Paxton asked. We were already on our way back to his house and since no one could see us, I opened up the envelope. Inside there were five little transmitters. I already knew we were supposed to put them in things we would keep on us at all times.

"It's just the trackers," I said, pulling one out. Since I drove the Hummer around, I placed one under the seat, just in case. That left us two each to put on our person.

"Okay, so that leaves two for you and two for me. Make sure you hook them on something you'll have on you at all times."

I sealed up the envelope and put it back in my bag, so they were secure until we got to Paxton's house. It was closing in on midafternoon and still no word from Cliff. I was worried about him.

"What's wrong?" Paxton asked.

I pulled out my phone and texted him again. "Cliff still hasn't gotten back to me."

He sighed. "Do you want to ride by the apartment and see if he's there? We can check out yours as well."

"Yeah, let's do that."

Paxton turned the Hummer around and started toward my place. My nerves were shot. I had no clue what we were going to find, and I prayed it wasn't going to be anything bad. Knowing my luck, it would be.

Paxton drove us into the parking lot. "Fuck," I hissed. "His truck isn't here."

After we parked, Paxton and I both got out and went straight for the stairs. "Just because his truck isn't here, doesn't mean he's not." When we got up to the third floor, I rushed straight to his door and knocked. A minute went by and I knocked again. Nothing.

Paxton put his arm around me. "Come on, Gabby, he's not here. Let's go check out your apartment and get out of here."

Reluctantly, I let Paxton lead the way. Luckily, there was nothing amiss at my door. No notes or black roses. I half expected to see a dead cat, or a horse head hanging by my door. Since Rage got his name for a reason I could see him taking his anger out on animals. I bet he killed them when he was younger. What made me sick was, people actually did that shit and enjoyed it.

When we got inside, everything seemed to be in place. It was strange being back there, since I hadn't really been by in a while. Oddly enough, it didn't feel like home anymore.

"Does everything look okay?" he asked.

The bananas on the counter were brown and mushy, so I threw them in the trash. "Yeah, it looks the way I left it. Let me check my room and then we can go."

As soon as I hit the hallway, I knew something was wrong. The door to my bedroom was shut. I hadn't left it like that. Paxton stopped and stepped in front of me. "What's wrong? You tensed up all of a sudden."

I nodded toward my room. "I didn't shut my door. Someone else did that."

Paxton's gaze narrowed and he pushed me back toward the kitchen. "You stay here. I'm going to check it out."

Instead of arguing, I nodded and let him go. While I was at it, I went and locked the front door. Nervously, I stood there tapping my foot, waiting to hear Paxton say something. When he called for me, I rushed back there. Inside my room, everything looked the same. My bed was made, the blinds were down, and everything was still on my . . .

"Something's missing," I pointed out. There was a spot on my dresser where a framed picture used to sit. You could even see the empty spot where the dust had collected around it. Someone had come in and taken it.

"What was it?"

"A picture of me and Ashleigh," I growled. "And that fucker stole it." I remembered the day we took it. Ashleigh and I were at the beach with Colin and Bradley. Colin was the one who took the photo because we were covered in seaweed. It was my favorite picture. "So help me God, this shit needs to end. I can't imagine what would've happened if I was here."

"Do you see anything else missing?" he asked. Paxton walked around my room, but I knew he wouldn't know if anything went missing. My heart sank when I noticed my jewelry box, moved to a different spot. When I opened it, there was indeed a ring missing. It was my high school graduation ring.

"He has a ring too," I hissed low, slamming the box closed. "There's no telling what all he took. He probably took some of my underwear. Sick bastard."

Paxton put his hands on my shoulders and squeezed. "We'll get your stuff back. I'm going to make this fucker pay for what he's done."

I traced the place where my picture used to sit. I was going to make him pay too.

CHAPTER 28

Gabriella

BY THE TIME we got back to Paxton's house, Mason had called back with an update. I put him on speakerphone so Pax could listen in while I made us club sandwiches.

"My guys are looking up information on Josh Davenport. I should have something on him later tonight."

"Speaking of him," Paxton spat, "it looks like he broke into Gabby's apartment and took some of her things."

"It's escalating, sooner than we expected. Thank fucking God she wasn't there," Mason thundered. "After studying the timeline, I think it's what you thought all along. When this guy sees you two together, it sets him off. Take for instance, the night at the race. He knew what you two were doing in the announcer's box and then the next day they want you to fight."

"So what do you suggest?" I asked. "If he watched us today all he saw us do was go to the gym and to my apartment."

"Or are you saying we need to do something scandalous?" Paxton cut in.

Mason chuckled. "Well, don't go off and start having sex in the middle of the Manhattan Beach pier or anything."

Paxton's eyes twinkled with mischief. "I think I have it. Leave it to me," he said. "I have the perfect idea to get him fired up."

"Just whatever you do, be careful. The sooner we get this mission done, the better. I don't like having to wait to kick ass. So do what you have to do and I'll call you back later with more details on Josh."

We said our goodbyes and Paxton jumped up and started toward the stairs.

"Where are you going? Don't you want to eat?" I was starving, so I took a bite of my sandwich and moaned when I swallowed it down.

"I'll be back in a minute. There's something I need to get. Keep in mind, after we eat, we have somewhere to go." He winked and darted up the stairs. By the time he made it down, I had already finished my sandwich and cleaned up the kitchen.

Paxton stuffed a huge bite of his sandwich in his mouth, smiling the entire time.

"What are you up to?" I asked curiously.

His grin grew wider. "I can't tell you, but whatever I do just go along with it, okay? I'm actually kind of curious to see your face when it all happens."

"Where are we going?"

"The beach," he replied. "Why don't you go and change clothes and by the time you get down, we'll be ready to go."

"Okay, but if you embarrass me today, I'm going to kick your ass." When all he did was laugh, I rolled my eyes and bolted up the stairs in search for my bathing suit. It was hidden in the drawer with all of the sexy lingerie I had yet to wear for Paxton. Maybe I could wear some tonight, if we weren't ass deep in trouble. Stripping out of my clothes, I put on my neon green bikini and covered up with a pair of denim shorts and a yellow tank top. I was ready to go.

Downstairs, Paxton had a cooler all packed up with waters and some snacks. His smile made my heart flutter when he watched me come down the stairs. I'd never felt like that before. "What beach are we going to? Are we going to stay around here?"

"I figured we could stay around here. Since the sun will be setting soon, we can walk up to one of the piers and back. If Rage isn't watching us, I'm pretty sure he'll find out what we did very quickly."

"Oh, dear God, I can only imagine what you're going to make me do," I laughed. "Well, let's go, the suspense is killing me." I was clueless, but also scared with how this was going to provoke Rage. This wasn't a game.

Paxton had a blanket set out beside the cooler, so I carried it while he handled the cooler. Once out of the back door, he locked it up and even locked the gate when we exited. We were going to be walking along a beach and we wouldn't be close by to see if anyone tried to get in. If Rage got into my apartment, there wasn't really anything stopping him from getting into Paxton's home.

Reaching the beach, Pax found a spot and stopped. "Let's set our stuff down and take a walk. We should be able to make it to the pier in thirty minutes or so."

Smiling, I spread our blanket on the sand, and he set the cooler down on top of it so it wouldn't blow away. "Sounds good to me. Lead the way." I held out my hand and he took it, pulling me in the direction of the pier. I could see it in the distance, but it was still a good little ways away.

Hand in hand, we strolled up the beach, letting the cool water rush across our feet. "I bet Ashleigh misses the ocean," I mumbled more to myself than anything.

"Probably, but she's happy with Ryley. If you're happy with who you're with, I believe you can be happy anywhere." He squeezed my hand. "There's something I want to tell you."

Furrowing my brows, I gaped up at him. "Uh-oh. Is this a 'we need to talk' moment? The way you said it makes it sound like I'm going to get pissed."

He chuckled lightly and kept walking. "Ashleigh hasn't told you that we talk, has she?"

"What do you mean *talk*? When?" She never told me anything about talking to Paxton. *Sly she-devil.*

"A couple times. For example, before we got started, she said you and I acted like her and Ryley did before they got back together."

"So this was her way of helping me?"

Lifting my hand, he kissed it and smiled. "Helping *us*, sunshine. She was the one who kept telling me you were interested. Why do you think I pushed so hard?"

"I don't know," I teased, "maybe it's because you're

a stubborn ass." I elbowed him in the side and he laughed.

"That's part of it, but I'm not the type of person to give up when I want something. Neither are you. She wanted to help you like you helped her and Ryley. I admire that in you, Gabriella. You love your friends and you protect them. There aren't many people in the world that are like that."

"Well, I know of one person like me," I said, turning to face him. We were finally at the pier and there were tons of people around, but all I could focus on was him. It was as if we were the only two people there. Backing myself against the post, I pulled him to me and wrapped my arms around his neck. "You're just like that too. It's not something you let everyone see, but it's there. I'm just glad you let me in. If not, I don't think we'd be here right now."

The wind blew a strand of hair in my face and he gently brushed it away. "I knew what I needed to do for you to see me. It was a sacrifice I had to make, which brings me to what I need to say next."

He leaned over and kissed me, but it wasn't chaste. I felt his need and his desire pour into my body, as if he was giving it to me. But most importantly, I felt his love. He might be scarred by the darkness he'd given in to once before, but he needed me and I sure as hell needed him. I couldn't imagine these days without him.

When he pulled his lips away, he rested his forehead to mine and kept his gaze on me while he pulled my hand down away from his neck. I didn't even ask what he was doing until I felt the cold metal slide down my finger.

Paxton got down on his knee. Wide-eyed, I gaped at him with my mouth wide open like a fish. Was he really proposing to me? Gasps erupted from the crowd of people around us. My heart thundered rapidly in my chest and I almost gave in to the hype, until I remembered this had to be his plan . . . the thing to drive Rage over the edge. It all made sense. If he thought Paxton and I were going to get married, he'd know we were serious; that I was definitely unattainable.

The flock of people closed in around us, taking pictures and videos. I even heard Paxton's name being murmured across the crowd. They knew who he was. Holding my hand in his, I looked down at the ring and my eyes watered. It was gorgeous, but it wasn't really mine. This was all fake. It was shiny and bright with diamonds all across the band, but the center stone sparkled in a majestic blue color, like the ocean.

"I love you, Gabriella Reynolds. I know we haven't been together long, but I've known what I wanted ever since the day I first saw you. Witnessing your love and passion for the things you do and the people you love encouraged me to do the same. It's because of you I want to be a better man—that I *am* a better man. I don't think I can ever let you go." Then his hand squeezed mine and his green gaze penetrated straight through to my soul. My knees grew weak and I held my breath. I knew what was coming next.

"I want you to be my wife, Gabby. Tell me you'll say yes."

"Yes," the ladies around us prodded. "Say yes."

Paxton chuckled, but never swayed his eyes from mine. "What do you say, sunshine? Do you think you can put up with me for the rest of your life?"

"If she doesn't, honey, I'll be more than happy to," an

old lady shouted.

"Yes," I cried, nodding my head. "The answer's yes."

Jumping to his feet, Paxton picked me up in his arms and twirled me around. The crowd cheered and screamed in delight as we kissed and held each other. Everyone who walked by gave us their congratulations and well wishes. As far as proposals went, it was pretty damn epic.

After the excitement died down, we started on our way back down the beach to his house. I tried not to stare at the ring on my finger, but it fit perfectly, like it was made for me. "I have to say, you did that very convincingly," I confessed. "You definitely had me believing it."

Paxton smiled, looking down at the sand. "I'm pretty sure Rage will find out about it if he doesn't already know."

"The ring is beautiful. Is it a sapphire?" I asked, holding my hand up. It twinkled as the last rays of the sun shone across the water.

"Actually, it's a diamond. It was my mother's."

I gasped, holding my hand over my heart. "Oh my God," I breathed. We finally made it back to his house, but his mood had shifted. "Paxton, we need to get inside so I can take it off. I don't want anything happening to your mother's ring."

I expected him to laugh and shrug it off, but there was no humor in his face when he gazed down at me. I shivered when he took my face in his hands. "I like it where it's at, Gabriella. If you want to take it off that's fine, but I think it looks good on your hand. Besides, we're engaged now. We need to act like it."

"So what exactly do engaged couples do?" I teased, lifting up on my toes. I bit his bottom lip and sucked it between my teeth.

Groaning, he pressed his body to mine and I felt his cock respond. "I can think of a million things."

About that time, both of our phones rang, slicing through our tension. He looked down at his and I looked down at mine. "Who's calling you?" I asked.

"My cousin. You?"

"Ashleigh," I laughed. "So how long do we need to play this off?"

"For as long as you want, sunshine." He kissed me quickly and answered his phone. *For as long as I want?* How was I supposed to handle a question like that? Being prepared, when I answered the phone I held it away from my ear knowing Ashleigh was going to squeal. Needless to say, she did.

"Hey, Ash," I greeted once her screams died down. "How are you?"

"How am I? How are *you*? There are videos going around everywhere of Paxton proposing. How the hell did that happen?"

I watched Paxton as he talked to his cousin and when his eyes met mine, something changed. We took a step without meaning to, and it was both scary and exhilarating. Life was never going to be the same.

"Ashleigh, to be honest, I've never been better. I love him."

"See, I knew you were hot for him. And now look at you happy lovebirds. You can live happily ever after."

Little did she know, our lives weren't a fairy tale. We were stuck in a hell that I could only pray we'd get out of unscathed. Until then, I had to pretend all was okay.

"Yes," I murmured. "Our own little fairytale."

CHAPTER 29

Gabriella

THE WHOLE EVENING was spent talking to people on the phone and hearing everyone's congratulation spiels. My brother even called, but I wasn't ready to talk to him. He wouldn't understand and I couldn't tell him about the mission we were working on. For now, I had to keep him in the dark, just like everyone else.

Thankfully, by ten o'clock the calls had slowed down and we both had time to take a quick rinse off and change clothes. I opted for a pair of pink pajama shorts and a white cami, which Pax loved. He groaned when his phone started to ring again, so he shut it off and threw it across the room. I wished I could do that to mine, but I just couldn't. Grabbing my brush off the bathroom counter, I sauntered into the bedroom and sat down beside Paxton on the bed. The wind did a number on my hair, so I took a deep breath and started brushing out the knots.

"I knew the news would travel, but I didn't think it would go that fast." Paxton shook his head. Taking the brush from my hand, his fingers lingered over the ring for a moment before trailing down my arm.

Gently, he stroked the brush through my hair and my breath hitched. It felt so good. Even more so when he brushed the hair off my shoulder and placed his lips on my bare skin. "What did you expect?" I whispered huskily. "You're Paxton Emerson, a sexy as hell fighter every female would give up just about anything to be with."

"Would you give up everything to be with me?"

My eyes fluttered closed as his fingers worked through my hair and then down my back. "There's nothing I wouldn't do to keep you."

Deftly, he slid his hands up my shirt and reached around to my breasts, squeezing them. My breasts felt heavy and sensitive as he rolled my nipples between his fingers, pinching them to make me squirm. "Do you want something, Mr. Emerson?"

"You . . . only you." Laying me back, he came from behind and covered me with his body. He traced my lips with his tongue and pushed his cock against my center. "It's only ever going to be you."

The second his lips touched mine and I closed my eyes, my damn phone rang. Paxton froze against my lips and groaned, sliding off of me so I could get it. "This is really starting to piss me off," he grumbled.

"Tell me about it." But when I peered down at the phone, I knew I had to take it. "It's Scar," I said. Paxton bolted upright, his expression hard when I answered the phone. "Yeah."

"Yeah, is right," Scar countered. "You know, I told you to calm it down with Reaper, but you just couldn't do that could you?"

"I agreed to three fights, not to change my whole life around. You don't own me," I spat. Paxton's nostrils flared and he clenched his hands into tight fists. He was itching to have it out with Scar.

"I may not own you, but there's still one more fight you owe me. Rage wanted to bring you in tonight, but there wasn't enough time to plan."

"Tomorrow then?"

"Yes."

He hadn't mentioned anything about Paxton fighting, so I assumed it was something he didn't want known. I had to play it off. "Good, I can beat the next fucker down and you can get the hell out of my life. Then Rage can kiss my ass and go stalk somebody else." I would rather him stalk me than some helpless woman. All in all, they needed to be stopped.

"Same time, same place. Don't be late." The line went dead.

Snarling, I stared at my phone. "What a jackass."

"What did he say?" Paxton inquired.

I set my phone down on the nightstand and laid back. "He didn't say anything about you. I guess it's supposed to be a surprise."

"You don't think Camden would lie to us do you?"

"No," I stated adamantly. He'd fucked over his brother and my best friend and I wanted to kill him for it, but out of all of his friends, I was there for him. I never judged him or Ryley when everyone else around them did. They were my friends.

"Camden doesn't belong with Scar," I murmured. "He may be a self-centered pain in the ass, but he's not fully gone. The Camden I met a long time ago is still in there. I just don't know what it's going to take to get him to change."

Paxton clasped my chin and rubbed his thumb over my lips. "I've been there too, sunshine. It takes a certain person to come along, and right now, he doesn't have that."

A text came through my phone and I jumped. Paxton and I both groaned. "Let's see who it is, shall we?" I grumbled sarcastically, reaching for my phone. Speak of the devil.

Camden: Just got word. The fight is definitely on.
Camden: Tell Emerson to be ready for anything.

Handing the phone to Paxton, he read the messages then got out of bed.

"Where are you going? It's late," I exclaimed.

His body was coiled tighter than a snake. He was already in the zone. There would be no reasoning with him being like that. "I have to be ready, sunshine. There's no way in hell I could sleep anyway."

After watching him throw on a pair of shorts and T-shirt, he stormed out of the room. Quickly, I got out of bed and followed him. "Well, I'm not letting you do this alone. I'll help you."

With his back to me, he opened the front door and stopped. "You need your rest, Gabby. This is going to be just as hard on you as it is on me."

"That's true, but you must be forgetting something." I came up behind him and wrapped my arms around his waist. "You see this ring you put on my finger?" He looked down and placed his hand over mine. "It may just be for show, but it means we stand together through the good and bad. You're in this shit because of me. Let me help you."

Taking my hand, he lifted it to his lips and kissed my palm. Without any more words, he pulled me out the door and straight to his garage. It was going to be a long night.

CHAPTER 30

Paxton

FOR HOURS, I trained nonstop and envisioned Scar and that fucker Rage every time I hit the bag. I was accustomed to fighting ruthlessly, but there was nothing at stake other than my own life. It wasn't like that now. I wasn't fighting for justice, or to teach someone a lesson. I was fighting for Gabby, to keep her safe.

While I trained, she called Mason to tell him the fight was on. He promised his team would be ready. We both had our trackers in place so each one of us had two. Mason tested them out and they were all set to go.

Gabriella kept up with me until three in the morning, but then passed out on the mat. I didn't want to carry her into my house without me there, so I covered her with a couple of towels and rolled one up to put under her head.

The thought that I was going to leave her at the mercy of Scar and Rage tonight terrified the shit out of me. I didn't want her out of my sight. Unfortunately, we had no choice. When her phone rang and I noticed it was Mason, I silenced it and quietly rushed downstairs.

"Mason, what's up?" I answered. "Anything new?"

"Thank fucking God *you* answered. I tried calling your phone."

After getting phone call after phone call it had started to piss me off. "I turned it off after everyone wouldn't leave us alone. Apparently, our engagement circulated a lot faster than I anticipated."

Mason chuckled uneasily. "I saw that. Nice touch by the way. However, after what I found out about Josh Davenport, we might've taken this a little further than we needed."

"What are you talking about?"

He cleared his throat. "It looks like this Josh character is seriously fucked up in the head. He's wanted for killing not one, but three girls in the past two years, as well as two men. Looking at the reports, he stalks them before he makes his move. The first two women were obsessions. When they didn't submit to him, he killed them. One had a boyfriend and he killed him too."

"What about the other guy?" I asked. "Who was he?"

"Now this next instance is a different story. Josh was actually dating this victim, but when he walked in on her and another man, he flipped out. And I'm not talking just a bullet to the brain. I'm talking straight up bloody and psychotic as fuck. He dismembered them completely."

"I'm assuming you don't want Gabby knowing all of this?" I asked.

Mason sighed. "Not exactly the details, but after the whole engagement fiasco and with the way this guy is, I think it might be good if she doesn't flaunt the idea in front of him. If she does, he might snap and take it out on her. That's the last thing we want."

"So what exactly are you saying?"

"You're not going to like this, but I'm saying that if this guy comes for her, she can't fight him. I know it's going to be against all her instincts, but we can't take any chances."

"What if he tries to touch her? Am I supposed to just let him?" I hissed.

"Paxton, I've been in this same situation before. I had to watch someone else kiss Claire right in front of me. Did I want to kill him? Yes. But I had to concentrate on the objective, and that was getting her out of there and keeping her safe. This isn't just about you and Rage, it's about Gabriella. Don't forget that."

"I won't." There was no way in hell I could forget it.

"If you can, text me before everything goes down. If you can't, I'll keep watch of the trackers to see where it leads us."

"Will do."

"Is Gabriella asleep?"

I looked up the stairs to the open door of my gym. Her still form was lying on the floor, unmoving. "She passed out a while ago."

"Tell her I'll call her later. I want to go over everything with her before it all goes down."

"I will."

"And be careful, both of you. Try to get some rest. You're going to need it."

"Don't I know it," I grumbled. After we hung up the phone, I trudged up the stairs and laid on the floor with Gabriella. Her eyes fluttered open and she snuggled into my side before closing them again.

"I can't believe I fell asleep. Do you forgive me?" she asked, yawning.

Putting my arm around her, I closed my eyes and held her tight. "Don't worry, sunshine. You're going to make it up to me once all of this is over."

Her breathing slowed and she smiled. "I look forward to it."

CHAPTER 31

Gabriella

PAXTON'S DEEP BREATHING was all I focused on until the sun came up, shining through the small window. I didn't want to move and wake him up, so I stayed there while he slept. His arms were covered in tattoos from his shoulders down to his wrists and intermingled around the celtic symbols was the skull tattoo that gave him access to the Dark Side. I never noticed it before, but *Reaper* was printed just inside of it. I traced it lightly.

"What are you doing?"

"I was just looking at your tattoos. Does everyone have to get the skull if they want to be a part of the underground shit?"

He looked down at his arm. "Yes. And trust me, I'd take it back if I could."

Stretching my arms, I sat up and looked for my phone. It wasn't beside me. "Do you know where my phone is?"

Paxton slipped it out of his back pocket and handed it to me. "Mason called while you were sleeping, so I answered it."

I took it from him. "What did he say?"

"I tell you what," he said, getting to his feet. He held out a hand and I took it so he could lift me up. "How about we spend this day *not* talking about tonight? I think we need to concentrate on the good in our lives."

"What do you suggest?" I asked.

Instead of answering, he gazed down at me with those sea green eyes of his, the intensity making me tremble. Sliding his fingers underneath my cami straps, he pulled them down my shoulders and over my breasts, exposing my bare flesh. His kisses started on my lips and trailed down my neck, only to stop at my sensitive peaks. He was on his knees now, staring up at me as he sucked my nipple into his mouth. My legs grew weak, but he held me tight, licking his way down my stomach as he lowered my shirt and shorts past my hips to the floor.

I dropped to my knees and let him guide me down on the mat. He covered me with his body, keeping his gaze on mine as he thrust deliciously hard. No words were said, it was just our bodies moving together. The perfect sound. Holding my body tight, he picked up the pace, his grunts deep and hot as his breath hit my ear. His grip was almost painful, but yet I held him with just as much need. I was close to losing control. Wrapping my legs around his waist, I squeezed them hard and rocked my hips.

Taking my face in his hands, he pulled my bottom lip

between his teeth—the pleasure and pain of it sending me over the edge. My body tightened around him at the same time he released inside me. We laid there connected and in each other's arms for what felt like only seconds, but it ended up being hours. No words, just us.

Once Paxton and I decided to separate from each other, I chose to take a shower and relax while he continued with his brutal training. There actually wasn't any relaxing going on, but I had to at least pretend everything was right in the world. If only for a couple of hours. Sitting by the window, I could see Paxton in his garage staring off into space. I could only imagine what was going through his mind.

I had two hours before I needed to be at my apartment and still no one had gotten in touch with Paxton to tell him he was going to fight. We had no clue who was going to come for him. When Ryley had to fight, it was Scar who showed up at the arena.

My phone vibrated. "Hey, Mason," I answered, keeping my focus on Paxton.

"Did Paxton tell you I called?"

"Yes, but he didn't tell me what you talked about."

He sighed. "Look, Gabby, tonight is gonna be no joke. I've dealt with these kinds of people before and they're hardcore. Most likely, someone's going to get hurt. I mean seriously hurt. I just want you to be prepared."

"I'm ready, Mason. You know I'm strong."

"And here's where I need you to be stronger," he began. "Rage isn't just going to settle for this fight with Paxton. He wants you, win or lose. What I want from you is your full cooperation."

"What do I need to do?" I asked.

"If something happens and Rage gets his hands on you, I want you to play along. If you fight and tell him to fuck off, it's going to piss him off. Not to mention, right now he thinks you're engaged. Don't provoke him. I've seen his record and he doesn't take very kindly to rejection."

Dread settled into the pit of my stomach. "What if he tries to rape me?"

"That's when you fight, Gabby. Whatever happens, I'm going to be close. Are you ready for this?"

No, but I had to be.

CHAPTER 32

Gabriella

I HAD TEN minutes left before I needed to leave. Paxton thundered up the steps and when he got to the room, his deep breaths were all I could hear.

"What are you doing?" he asked, coming up behind me. I took the ring off my finger and gently set it on his dresser. "I talked to Mason. The last thing Rage needs to see is the ring on my finger. Besides, I don't want anything to happen to it." It was strange, but I didn't want to take it off. I'd only worn it for one day, but it felt like it was a part of me. "Has Camden or anyone called you yet?" I asked, turning around.

He was on edge, his fists clenched tight and his jaw firm. "No. And they probably won't until you're gone."

This was it. This was what we dreaded . . . having to

say goodbye. Stepping around him, I grabbed my bag, making sure I had my phone and plenty of money in case I needed it.

"You know, I thought I could handle you leaving, but not knowing what's going to happen is totally fucking with my head. My instinct is to keep you here and fight every motherfucker who tries to come after you."

"And I know you would," I murmured wholeheartedly, glancing at the clock. "It's time, Pax. I have to go." Taking me in his arms, he held me tight, crushing me. I squeezed my eyes shut to keep the tears at bay; I had to be strong. "It'll all work out. Mason's ready and so is his team. Just be careful."

"You too, sunshine. I'll see you when this is all over." His lips pressed into mine and I opened for him, tasting him desperately. I breathed him in and put it all to memory.

Before he decided to keep me hostage, I broke away from the kiss. "I love you."

Sighing, he rested his forehead to mine. "And I love you."

Clutching my bag, I bolted out of his room and down the stairs. I was going to be late. The Hummer was in the driveway, ready for me. I tossed my bag inside and hopped in. When I pulled out of the driveway, I made the mistake of looking back in the mirror. Paxton was by his front door with his hands in his hair. The tormented look on his face made my heart break. Hopefully it would all be over soon.

The whole way to my apartment, I sped like a bat out of hell. When I pulled into the parking lot, I half expected to see Camden's sports car there, but unfortunately, it was Red. Groaning, I pulled up beside him and rolled my window down. "Where's Camden?" I asked.

Red grinned and opened my door. "Sorry to disappoint, sugar tits, you got me tonight."

Before getting out of the car, I rolled up the window and turned it off. I had hoped Cliff would be out there somewhere, but I didn't see him. "What happened to my friend?" I asked.

Red took my bag and opened my door. "That's none of your business. Get in." Once I got inside, he slammed the door and went around to his side. He didn't even bother looking in my bag this time; he just threw it in the back. *Damn, I should've brought a gun.* "You know the drill," he said, passing me a blindfold.

I had never noticed it before, but on his forearm was the skull tattoo. And right below it had his name . . . Malice.

CHAPTER 33

Paxton

GABRIELLA HAD ONLY been gone twenty minutes when Camden showed up at my doorstep. My stomach clenched. I had hoped he would be the one with Gabriella. "Who's with Gabby?" I snapped as soon as I opened the door.

He shrugged. "I'm not sure. Scar told me to come get you and if I had to use force then I was more than welcome. But they knew I wouldn't have to once I told you they had Gabriella."

"Is that it? You don't know anything else?"

Camden shook his head. "They've kept pretty quiet about this whole thing. I think they're up to something. I just don't know what."

That wasn't what I wanted to hear. "All right, let me

get my bag. I'm ready to get this shit over with."

As soon as I had my things, I met Camden out at his car and got in. In my seat was a blindfold. I was an outsider now. Once I put it on, Camden started on the way. "Why are you helping us?" I asked curiously. "You never help anyone but yourself."

He chuckled. "And you're right. I'm only doing this for Gabby. She may be a pain in the ass with a big mouth, but she doesn't deserve to be put at the hands of someone like Rage. No one does. As soon as all of this is all over, it's right back to my usual self."

"Great," I mumbled. "You know, I used to be just like you. It gets kind of lonely after a while, does it not?"

"Nope, I like my life."

He said it, but I didn't believe a word. One of these days, he'd come around. Even Kyle seemed to be different when I talked to him. For the rest of the ride, it took about thirty minutes. I didn't exactly trust Camden, so I was glad we never told him about Mason and the plan.

"We're here." He came around to my side of the car and opened the door. "Once we're inside, I'm going to take you to Scar."

"Will Gabby be there?"

"I don't know. It looks like Malice's truck is missing. He must be the one who had to get her."

"Shouldn't they be here by now?" Camden's silence was answer enough and I didn't like it.

"Come on, let's go. I'll find her."

We started moving and once inside the doors, it was silent. Camden removed the blindfold and I followed him down a long hallway until we got to a door. Inside was Scar with two of his goons. I recognized them from before when I used to fight. Their names were Sniper and Slade. They disposed of the people who broke the rules.

"Reaper, good to see you again. I guess Striker didn't need to twist your arm to come."

Snarling, I stepped inside his office and went straight to his desk. "Where's Gabby?" I wanted to beat the smirk off his face and snap his fucking neck. Scar never fought in the ring and I'd give anything to take him out. I wouldn't think twice about killing him or Rage.

"Oh, don't worry, she's safe. If you win the fight, you'll get to see her again. If not, then it looks like you won't be seeing anyone ever again."

"So what are you saying? We're fighting to the death?"

His smile grew wider. "That's what Rage wants and since you turned your back on us, I think it's only fitting. Besides, he wants your girl and he's made it abundantly clear that he's not going to stop until he gets her."

Darting for his neck, I didn't get far before Camden's arm draped around my body and Sniper's gun pointed straight at my head. Breathing hard, I held out my arms, signaling my surrender. The gun lowered and Camden let me go.

"Rage isn't going to touch her," I hissed, pinning a lethal glare his way. "If he does, you both die." The Reaper was back. And this time, I'd finish the job myself.

Scar chuckled and dismissed me with a wave of his hand. "Striker, take him away. The fight starts in fifteen minutes."

Camden opened the office door and I stalked out, my pulse thundering out of control. I knew where I was about to go. "Dude, calm down," he hissed.

I followed him down the hall to another door. Inside, was a chair and nothing else but a small window on the door the bidders could look through. Clenching my teeth, I marched inside. "I'd like to see you stay calm if it was *your* girl you were fighting to keep safe. But then again, you'll probably never know what that's like."

Camden stood by the door and started to close it, his expression unreadable. "Probably not, but you need to focus. Make sure you put this fucker down. I'm going to try and find Gabby."

CHAPTER 84

Gabriella

SOMETHING WASN'T RIGHT. The smell of the air, everything was off. Red firmly held my arm and pulled me along, but instead of cement beneath my feet, it was grass. There wasn't supposed to be grass. "Where are we?" I asked. My body screamed for me to run, that danger was ahead.

Digging my feet into the ground, I tried to jerk out of his hold and lift the blindfold over my head, but his grip tightened even more. "Relax. We just took a little detour."

"A detour? What the fuck are you talking about? I'm supposed to be fighting."

I walked up a couple of steps and then a door creaked. "Not tonight you're not, but we do get to watch it."

He helped me inside and the place smelled musty,

like no one had been there in a while. "Watch it? I don't understand."

The ominous chuckle that escaped his lips made the hair on the back of my neck stand straight up. "You'll see, sweetheart. It's going to be fucking epic."

He pushed me down in a chair and before I could relax my arms, he pulled them behind me and bound my wrists together. "What the fuck are you doing?" I tried to jerk free, but it was no use. I couldn't move and I couldn't see. However, it didn't stop there. When he started on one of my ankles, I panicked. Instinctively, I jerked up with my knee and clocked him in the nose.

"Stupid bitch," he growled, slapping me across the cheek. My head snapped to the side and my eyes watered. It hurt like hell, and unfortunately, it caught me off guard. He used my hesitation to his advantage and finished tying me down. Now, I was completely at his mercy, or anyone else who decided to come along.

"You're going to pay for that," I hissed low. "I think it's pretty pathetic you have to tie me up. Are you afraid I'm going to escape?"

"Hardly," he scoffed. "Now shut the fuck up." Before I could come up with a reply, he left the room. My bag was still in his truck, so hopefully, the trackers would lead Mason and his team here. There had to be someone close by. Red came back in, and it sounded like he was setting something up in front of me.

It wasn't until he lifted my blindfold that I saw what he was doing. It took a few seconds to adjust to the light and it didn't help that my face stung. The room we were in was a living room with ratty navy furniture and smoke stained walls. I could even smell the stale stench of cigarettes in the musty, moldy air. There were no windows, but over Red's shoulder I could see the kitchen . . . and a door. One way or another, I was going to escape out of that door. Red fiddled around with a laptop and once the video came into focus he set it down on the table.

"Are you ready for the show?"

Swallowing hard, I bit the inside of my cheek to keep from speaking. Dread settled in the pit of my stomach and the bile rose to the back of my throat, gagging me. The screen showed the fighting ring I recognized all too well. Two people were battling it out and blood was everywhere. There was no sound to the video and I was almost thankful I couldn't hear the screams.

Averting my gaze, I turned to Red who watched on in fascination. *Disgusting maggot.* Why couldn't *he* be in the ring getting the shit beat out of him? It didn't take a genius to figure out what we were about to look at next. After this fight, it was going to be Paxton and Rage. They didn't want me there so they could mess with Paxton's head. Taking a deep breath, I closed my eyes.

"You're not falling asleep are you? The most exciting part of the evening is coming up," Red mentioned.

My eyes snapped open and I glared at him. "I don't get off on watching people hurt and kill each other. Now, if it was you in the ring, I might have a different opinion."

"Trust me, I've done some damage in there, but tonight isn't about me. It's about you."

By the time I looked back at the screen, the fight was already over. I had no clue if anyone was killed, and I didn't want to know. By the amount of blood on the mat, I'd say someone met their maker. Three men, dressed in hooded robes, sprayed off the mat with water hoses like nothing ever happened. Even through the screen I could smell the blood. Knowing Paxton was about to enter that same ring terrified the shit out of me.

"Here we go," Red announced excitedly.

Keeping my eyes glued to the screen, I stared helplessly as I watched Paxton enter the ring, confident and completely pissed off. With his body tense and ready to kill, he was almost unrecognizable. The camera was set back a little too far, but it didn't take away from the murderous gleam in his eyes.

Without me there, I was afraid of what he would do. But when the door to the cage opened and three men ventured inside, it no longer mattered what he would do . . . it was what they were going to do to him.

"Oh, my God."

"That's right, sugar tits. You might want to watch because this will be the last time you see lover boy alive."

CHAPTER 35

Paxton

"IT TAKES THREE of you cowards to fight me?" I snapped angrily. Scar was by the door, blocking it, while I was surrounded by the three cocksuckers. One had on a black hood, while the other two were ready to fight. A thick set of chains dangled from one of the fighter's hands, and the other had brass knuckles with spikes.

Camden had yet to come into the room with Gabriella, which infuriated me more. I needed to see her, to make sure she was okay. If not, every motherfucker in the room was going to feel my wrath.

"No, I think two will suffice," the one in the hood spoke.

"Who the fuck are you?" I asked. Judging by the malevolence pouring off him, I had no doubt who he was . . .

and I was going to kill him. At least that way, I would know for a fact he couldn't go after Gabby.

He chuckled, but kept his face hidden. I wanted to know who the fuck he was; his voice was familiar. "You know who I am. I'm the one who's going to walk right out of here and go straight to your girl. Someone has to console her after she finds out your dead."

Growling, I lunged forward, but was stopped when both of the other fighters grabbed a hold of me. Rage laughed and stalked forward. "You're not going to touch her, you psycho ass motherfucker. I'm not going to let you hurt her like you did the other women you stalked, harassed, and killed."

"Those bitches had it coming. They fucked me over and paid the price. However, I don't plan on hurting Gabriella at all, if she submits to me. You see, she's different. I could see it in her eyes that she wants me. If it wasn't for you, I'd already have her. Once you're out of the way, she'll be mine." Turning on his heel, he headed for the cage door.

"So you're a pathetic coward then," I spat. "It's funny because I thought you were going to fight me on your own. I guess you're scared of the Reaper."

He stopped mid-step, his hands clenched at his sides. Slowly, he turned around and I could smell his anger permeating the room. I needed him to stay in the ring, at least until Mason and his people got into place. "I'm not scared of you," he growled low. "I'd just rather be fucking my girl than being here, wasting my time with you. Farewell, Reaper."

Scar opened the door and before Rage could stroll out, I head butted the guy behind me, breaking his nose, and punched the other in the side of the head. All I could see was red as I charged toward Rage. Still, it wasn't fast enough before the cage door was slammed in my face— Rage on the other side, walking away.

Scar smirked. "It's been good having you around Reaper, but your time is up."

I heard the chains being whipped into the air only mere seconds before pain exploded in my head. Blood oozed down my neck and back, but I couldn't focus on the pain. Rage exited the room and I knew it was only a matter of time before Gabriella would be in his grasp.

CHAPTER 36

Gabriella

"DAMN, DID YOU see that hit?" Red blurted excitedly. "I bet he's got one hell of a headache right now."

I'd seen the hit and it made me sick. Screaming for Paxton to turn around, tears welled in my eyes when he took the hit.

"I'm kind of bummed though. Rage was supposed to murder his ass."

"That was Rage who left?" I asked, stomach clenching. I was hoping it wasn't him.

Red nodded. "He's probably on his way to you. He's been hard up for you ever since Vegas."

Holy fuck. What was I going to do? "How far away are we from there?"

Red huffed and grabbed my chin, turning it to the television. "That's none of your concern. Now watch the damn fight."

When I tried to jerk out of his hold, he clenched down harder, keeping my face in the direction of the laptop. Fighting off two men with weapons wasn't easy, and every minute that passed by, I could see Paxton slowly begin to falter.

Where the hell was Mason? The guy with the spiky knuckles took a swipe at Pax and it sliced across his chest, blood oozing down. When Paxton stumbled, the fighter with the chains reared back and pummeled him on the side of the head. Paxton went down . . . and everything in my world shattered. I struggled to breathe, to think, as I sat there looking at his still form.

"Get up," I shouted as the tears welled in my eyes. Red laughed as both fighters circled the ring triumphantly. I ignored him and kept my focus on Paxton, my fighter. He had to get up, he just had to. There was no way in hell I was going to imagine being in a world without him.

"He's not getting up. He's done," Red chuckled victoriously. "That was too fucking easy."

Both fighters circled around Paxton's motionless body and moved closer and closer. *Come on, Pax. Get up.* My stomach clenched and when I thought I couldn't watch anymore, Red shut the lid closed, just as the other fighters were about to start beating him again.

"What are you doing?" I spat, tears blurring my vision. "I have to watch him get up. He needs to get up." Fighting against my restraints, my skin burned with my struggles and I didn't care. I had to get out of there.

Red jumped to his feet and grabbed the tape, ripping off a piece and slapping it over my mouth. "You just don't know when to shut up, do you? Now fucking be quiet. Someone's here." Quietly, he crept out of the room and disappeared.

Please tell me it's Mason. I tried to stay quiet so I could listen, but nothing could prepare me for what I heard next. The gunshot was so loud my ears rang, followed by the loud thud of a body hitting the floor.

Squeezing my eyes shut, I shivered and broke into tears. A warm hand gently pulled the tape away from my mouth and tried to sooth me in a hushed voice. "Gabby, it's over. I'm getting you out of here."

The voice sounded so familiar and I thought I would never hear it again. Opening my eyes, I gasped as my savior's face came into view. "Oh my God . . . you're alive?"

CHAPTER 37

Paxton

I WAS HURTING and I was in pain, but I wasn't going to let anyone take me down. As I was lying on the mat waiting for the right time to strike, the sound of shouting and gunfire filled the underground dungeon.

Mason had finally come.

Scar opened the gate and shouted for his fighters to get out, but before they could escape, I jumped to my feet and tackled one of them to the ground. Scar glared at me with a murderous gleam and all I could do was smile when he turned around and landed face first into Camden's fist.

Ripping the chain from the fighter's hand, I wrapped it around his neck and pulled. He choked and gurgled, but I didn't care. I kept pulling. The room swarmed with officers and even Mason came into view and rushed over to

Camden who grappled with Scar.

Bending over, I hissed in the fighter's ear and tightened the chain. "I would give anything to hear your bones crack right now, to watch your life slip away in a matter of seconds. You don't deserve any mercy."

"Paxton, let him go," Mason called. Out of the corner of my eye, he slowly walked up the steps and into the cage with his arms spread out wide. My hands shook with the need to pull tighter, but thinking about Gabriella made me release him.

"You got lucky, shithead." Roughly, I let him go and got to my feet, kicking him in the face when I passed. Now he was out cold.

Rushing out, I found Scar on the ground with Camden holding his arms behind his back. "You're going to pay for this Striker. I don't like traitors," Scar warned.

Camden pulled Scar to his feet and roughly pushed him toward one of the officers. "You can pay me back all you want. I don't have anything to lose."

Once he was taken away, Mason holstered his gun and looked down at his watch. "Some people got away, but there's nothing we can do about that now. All we really need is this fucker," he said, glaring at Scar, "and Rage. But we have to go. Gabriella is in a house down the street and I just got word she's not alone anymore. My guys are surrounding the house."

I was already heading for the exit. "Then let's get the fuck out of here." I was covered in blood and my body ached, but nothing was going to stop me from killing that motherfucker if he'd so much as laid a finger on her.

CHAPTER 38

Gabriella

CLIFF WAS ALIVE. But now I needed to make sure Paxton was okay. "Cliff, I need you to open the laptop," I demanded. "I have to make sure Paxton's okay."

Looking at the computer, he sighed and opened it. When the live feed came to life, there was a body in the ring and I gasped. It was all blurry and I couldn't tell who it was. "Please tell me that doesn't look like Paxton," I pleaded. The guy had tattoos on his arms, but they didn't exactly look like Paxton's. Or did they? I couldn't rub my eyes to clear the tears away.

Cliff narrowed his gaze and focused on the screen. "I'm sorry, Gabby, but it doesn't look good." As soon as he said it, he shut the lid and I sobbed. How could it be possible? There was no way Mason would let that happen.

I needed a better look. Putting his arms around my shoulders, Cliff held me tight. "Shh . . . stop crying. We need to get away from here. If Scar finds us, we're both dead. We have to leave town."

I was in a daze, no longer here or there. If Scar wanted to find me, I wasn't going down without a fight. I refused to believe Paxton was gone. As soon as Cliff undid my hands, I rubbed my eyes. "I'm not going anywhere. Turn the video back on. I need to see if that was really Paxton."

Cliff shook his head and his gaze hardened. "You're coming with me, Gabby, end of story. And Paxton's dead. It's time to move on."

The way he looked and sounded, chilled me to the bone. It was cold, angry. I'd never seen him like that before. My instincts went on hyper alert, in fact they were screaming. Danger was nearby. "I thought you were dead," I whispered. "Where have you been?"

"Here," he answered. "Scar kept me here and made me fight for him. It was either that or die. I chose to live."

"Did you kill Red?" I asked.

"Red?"

"Malice. I never knew his name, so I called him Red."

Cliff cleared his throat and averted his gaze. His fingers lightly grazed my calves before slipping the knife against the tie, cutting it off. "I didn't know what else to do, Gabby. He left his gun on the counter, so I picked it up and shot him." His knuckles were torn open and raw, and it made me wonder . . .

"Did you have to kill other people too?"

He sighed, but then a small smile appeared before he

229

continued. He didn't think I saw it, but I did; chills ran down my skin. "I had no choice, Gabby. I did it to stay alive. But right now, I need to get you out of here before someone shows up."

My hands and feet were numb and tingly, but I could feel the blood rushing back into my appendages. However, something wasn't right. I could feel it in my bones. When I stood and stretched my legs, I saw something that made me freeze in terror.

On Cliff's back, right below his shirt line, was the Dark Side skull tattoo. All too quickly, Cliff got to his feet and slipped the knife back into his pocket, his shirt covering the mark. He reached for my hand, but I jerked back. Narrowing his gaze, the muscles in his jaw clenched when he held out his hand.

"We have to go, Gabby. There's no time to waste."

Swallowing hard, I took another step back. The door to the kitchen came into view and on the dirty tile floor I saw a puddle of blood. My attention was drawn up to a black hood sitting on the counter. I gasped and put a hand over my mouth. Cliff kept moving closer like a lion stalking its prey, his gaze hungry.

"Why?" I whispered.

"Why what?"

"Why me?"

A sinister smile splayed across his lips. "Why not you? You're a fighter and super hot. It'll be fun to break you. Besides, all I've wanted to do since Vegas is feel that tight pussy wrapped around my cock."

My heart sped rapidly and my breaths came out in pants. He wasn't going to break me and he sure as hell wasn't going to get his cock anywhere near my orifices. "I hate to disappoint you, *Rage,* but I don't break so easily."

In a lightning fast move, he lunged at me, but I jumped out of the way and rushed toward the kitchen. I didn't get far before he grabbed hold of my ankle and I face planted on the floor. However, I did get far enough into the kitchen to see Red, broken like a rag doll with a hole in his head.

Kicking my legs, I jammed my foot into Rage's nose and it started gushing. His fingers dug into my legs and with bruising force he pulled me under his body and secured my wrists with his hands. The air whooshed out of my lungs and I gasped, struggling to breathe as he kept his full weight on me.

"If we didn't have to leave, I'd fuck you right now." He was hard between his legs, pressing it into my thigh. That wasn't my only concern, because now he had his knife out and was caressing it against my skin. Starting at my cheek, he slid it down my neck, to the top of my shirt where he nicked my skin with the tip. Ever so carefully, he sliced my shirt down the center, exposing my bra and the blood welling on my chest.

"Just one taste and we'll go," he murmured, his gaze hungry for my blood. "That's all I want." His lips touched the mound of my breast and I wanted to fight him off, but I couldn't. He still had the knife out and if he'd killed people before, I knew I wasn't any different. I had to tread carefully. Moaning, he sucked the wound on my chest, humping my leg like a dog in heat. I had a feeling he wasn't going to stop with just one taste.

"Don't we need to go?" I asked through gritted teeth, hoping it would get his mind back on track.

He narrowed his gaze and looked down at me, licking

my blood off of his lips. "You're not going to fight me on this?"

Out of the corner of my eye, I saw movement at the kitchen window. Someone was there. I had to hope and pray it was the police. "No, I'm not going to fight. I prefer to keep my skin away from your knife."

His eyes twinkled when he looked down at my bare flesh. "I agree." He bent down and ran his tongue across my chest. "I look forward to seeing more of it."

Thankfully, he put his knife away and grabbed my wrists, hauling me up to my feet. I hissed when he gripped my arm and dragged me through the house after him. There was a set of stairs that led down into complete dark- ness and I had no choice but to follow. I couldn't see a thing.

"Where are we going?" I tried to keep my voice from shaking, but I failed.

His evil chuckle made me shiver. "No need to be afraid. My car's down in the basement. As soon as we're safely out of the states, we'll take a break."

Switching on the light, he let me go and tore the cover off of a brand new black Mercedes Roadster. Now that the light was on, I looked down at my torn shirt and crossed my arms. "I can't go out like this. My bag is in Red's truck."

He scoffed. "I'm not stupid. I bet your phone's in there too. I can't have you calling for help. As far as clothes, I have some from your apartment."

Psycho bastard. Did he honestly think his behavior was normal? "How are we going to get out of the states? Don't you need my passport?"

Grinning, he pressed the button on the wall and the

garage door lifted. "I had that taken care of a long time ago. One way or another, I was going to make sure you were with me."

Someone spoke from behind, "Isn't it a shame she won't be going with you."

Gasping, I turned around and locked eyes with Mason. Cliff instantly grabbed me around the neck with his knife held dangerously close to my artery. I swallowed and felt the stab of the blade in my skin.

Thankfully, it wasn't just Mason pointing a gun at Cliff's head. There were others, at least five of them. "Well, well, if it isn't Mason 'The Eagle' Bradley. I thought you retired from police work?" Cliff taunted.

"Not when it involves my family, dickhead. Or should I say, Josh Davenport. Let her go and back away slowly."

Cliff moved me back toward the Mercedes while Mason moved forward a step. "That's not going to work. If you and everyone else don't back the fuck up and let me be on my way, I'll slit her throat right here and now. I'm sure you know I'm capable of it."

Mason huffed and backed up a step, reluctantly lowering his gun and giving the signal for everyone else to follow. I mouthed the word 'Paxton' to him and he nodded reassuringly. It didn't matter where I was going or who I was with, as long as Pax was okay, I could get through anything. In fact, he slowly turned the corner and came into view, his gaze hardening the second he saw my torn shirt.

"Well, this just keeps getting better," Cliff grumbled. "So you turned into a pussy and called Mason for help. That's pathetic."

"I'd say it's a lot better than stalking women and killing them when they finally see you're a disgusting pile of shit."

Using his free hand, Cliff slid it up my thigh, and on up to my chest. "This one doesn't think I'm disgusting." He squeezed my breast hard. "In fact, she loves it when I touch her. Don't you, Gabby?" The knife dug harder into my skin and I hissed.

"Yes," I said through clenched teeth.

"Now that we got that settled, I want you all to back the fuck up."

I kind of hoped Mason would use his sharpshooting skills and just blast him through the head, but he didn't. Instead, they all backed away. With a pained expression, Paxton took a step back and disappeared.

Chuckling, Cliff bent down and whispered in my ear, "I guess ol' lover boy didn't like hearing your confession."

Biting my tongue, I kept my gaze on Mason until I was forced into the Mercedes. Were they seriously going to let me leave with him? Once Cliff got into the car, he backed it out of the garage and sped up the side driveway to the front of the house. There were police cars around, but they weren't blocking the road.

Revving the engine, Cliff pressed the gas as hard as he could and squealed the tires. My heart raced and I knew that if I was going to get out of there, I had to do something drastic. It just so happened that as soon as we left the driveway, the tires burst and the car clunked to the ground. As fast as I could, I grabbed the back of Cliff's head and slammed his face down into the steering wheel before opening the door. My foot got caught and I fell out onto the road. Before Cliff could get me in his grasp, Paxton came out of nowhere and jerked him out of the car.

"Gabby," Camden shouted. Rushing toward me, he grabbed my hand and pulled me away from the car.

"Thank God, you're okay," I cried, hugging him tight around the neck. When I tried to let go, he held me in place. "Camden, let me go." I pushed against his chest but he wouldn't budge.

"Trust me, Gabby, you don't want to see this." The sound of fists hitting flesh and the crunch of bones echoed through the night air. It was enough to make me sick.

"Why aren't they stopping this?" I screamed. The police were standing around, just watching it play out, with their guns pointed at the ground.

Camden held me tighter. "Let them handle this the way they want. That fucker deserves to get the shit beat out of him for what he's done."

"But he'll *kill* him," I cried. I didn't want that weight on Paxton's shoulders.

"Then he kills him, Gabby. Either way he's a dead man."

I grew lightheaded and nauseous. The sounds were too much. "I think I'm going to be sick." Immediately, Camden let me go and helped me down to the ground. It was then I got a glimpse of the fight.

The knife Cliff had earlier fell out of his hands when Paxton slammed his wrist into the pavement. Judging by the gashes on Pax's arms, he got a few good swipes in. However, it didn't faze him; he kept going. In fact, he reminded me of Ryley when he was in the ring with Camden. It was terrifying.

"Gabby, are you okay?" Mason asked, rushing to my side. Putting his hands on my shoulder, he looked down at the cut on my chest, eyes burning with hatred.

"I'm fine," I assured him. "He didn't do anything to me other than that. But please, Mason. I need you to stop Pax. *Please*."

My gaze drifted to Paxton who was now on top of Cliff, pounding his head into the pavement. Mason rushed off and desperately tried pulling him away, grunting with the force. Nostrils flaring, Paxton's eyes were wild and dangerous, his body shaking as he was torn away. He stared down at Cliff and nothing else, almost like he wasn't even there. It was the place where all of us fighters went while in the ring, but the place Paxton was in was much darker.

With all his strength, Mason held him steady until I could get over there. Slowly, I put my hands around Paxton's neck and turned him to face me. "Pax, look at me. It's over," I murmured.

He shook his head, still not looking at me. "It's not over until he's dead. I won't be able to rest until I know he's gone."

"He's never going to bother us again, I promise. Mason will make sure of that. Please, just look at me."

Huffing, he closed his cold eyes and stood there for a few minutes before opening them. Now they were sea green and crystal clear. Snaking his arms around my waist, he held me tight and lifted me in his arms. "I just wanted to keep my promise," he whispered.

"Which one?"

"The one where I said I would always keep you safe. I wanted to kill him, Gabby. I couldn't stop him from hurting you."

"Hey, I'm okay," I assured. "I'm a fighter too, remember? And you did keep your promise. You stopped him." Glancing over his shoulder, I think he did more than stop him. Cliff wasn't moving, and there was blood pooling underneath his head. Mason noticed my hesitation and came over.

"All right, I think it's time we all get out of here and head to the station. The others are going to go inside and look around. One of my men said they saw Josh, Cliff, or Rage, whatever the fuck you want to call him, pull the gun on the other one. I was also told they found some of the things he stole out of your apartment. We'll get all of that back to you once all of this is over."

Now that I thought about it, I didn't really want any of that stuff back, knowing Rage's hands had been all over them. The only thing I wanted was the picture he stole of me and Ashleigh. Paxton put his arm around me and guided me toward Mason's car, and Camden followed. It was still hard to wrap my head around the fact that Cliff was Rage the whole time. He's been living right beside me. I'd given him my number and *confided* in him about my stalker.

"Wait," I said, stopping mid-step. "My bag is in Red's truck. It has my phone in it."

Mason went to the truck and grabbed it before nodding to his car. Paxton opened the door and then slid in beside me, holding me close as Camden got in on the other side. Hopping in the driver seat, Mason quickly glanced at us and then started on the way.

I wasn't planning on looking back, but my curiosity got the better of me. The ambulance had pulled up and the paramedics were around his body, fingers checking for a pulse. Before the whole scene disappeared from view, I saw a white sheet billow in the wind as it was placed on top of Cliff's body.

He was dead. Paxton had killed him.

"After this is all over, I'm leaving town," Camden confessed.

I glanced over at him and Mason stared at him through the rearview mirror. "Why is that?" I asked. Paxton kept his gaze out the window, not saying a word.

"There will be severe repercussions for my actions. I'll have a price on my head. I'm not going to have a choice."

"So you're just going to leave? What about your friends? Your brother?"

Camden smiled, but it didn't reach his eyes. "I don't have any friends, Gabby. I think it's best if I turn around and never look back."

"But . . . it'll be lonely," I whispered, taking his hand.

He squeezed once and then let me go. "I'm used to it."

CHAPTER 39

Gabriella

Two Days Later

EVEN THOUGH IT had only been two days, it felt like an eternity. Paxton's house was just how we left it, including his mother's ring sitting on the dresser in my room. I didn't know if he still wanted me to wear it, but I put it on my finger anyway. It made me feel closer to him, especially since he wasn't talking to me.

When Paxton found out Rage was dead, I didn't know what to expect. For two days, we talked to the police and went through our stories over and over again. Paxton was held a lot longer than I had been, and at the end of the day, I could tell it was wearing on him. Hell, it was hard on us all, but Paxton couldn't seem to shake it.

"He's going through a lot right now," Mason explained, running his hands through his dark blond hair. His gaze focused on Paxton, and I could see his understanding.

Mason was heading back home and stopped in to see how we were doing. I hadn't left Paxton's side, even though he hadn't talked or looked at me since everything went down. I missed him, but I knew he needed his space. I would wait as long as I needed to.

"I know he is," I replied. "I just wish I could get him to talk to me."

Paxton was in the garage, working on his cars. The news stations had been by, hoping to get a glimpse of the local hero who helped solve a murder mystery. However, Paxton didn't view himself as a hero. No matter what everyone told him, it went in one ear and out the other.

Our story had spread throughout the country. Everyone knew how Mason busted up another underground fighting ring with the help of me and Paxton. I had briefly been afraid Paxton would lose his title for being involved, but it only brought him more fame. And now my title fight against Allie was receiving so much press and buildup, it scared the shit out of me.

Unfortunately, my brother wasn't too thrilled when he found out what we had done. Mason was the one who broke the news to him, and I was very thankful for that. Luckily, he was staying on vacation with his family. At least I didn't have to worry about facing him just yet.

Mason put his arm around me and squeezed. "It's not easy, but I know what the guy's going through. The first time I killed someone, it messed me up bad. Even though the guy pulled a gun on me first and I had no choice. It was my life or his. Still, it doesn't change the fact I did it . . . I ended someone's life."

"How do I help him?" I asked. I couldn't keep my eyes off of Paxton as he slaved away in his garage. For the past two days, I held in my tears but I couldn't do it anymore.

"I don't know if what I say is going to help, but it'll be a start. Do you want to know what Paxton said to me yesterday?" Crossing my arms, I glanced at him and nodded as a reply. "He said he wasn't sorry for killing Rage, that he most likely saved the lives of countless women by doing it. What he's most worried about is what you think of him now. You watched him kill another man. You saw a side of him that he didn't want you to see."

The tears streamed down my cheeks and I choked. "But I don't see him being any different. If I had the chance, I would've killed Rage. Nothing is going to change the way I feel about him."

Mason tapped me on the chin. "Then you should tell him that. Maybe he's afraid of seeing judgment in your eyes. Just let him know, no matter what, you will always be there through the good and the bad. He's at a low point, but you can bring him back up with your love and support. You can do this." Wrapping his arms around my waist, he embraced me one last time before getting in his car and nodding toward the garage. "Go get 'em. I'll see you at the title fight."

Mason waved once he got out of the driveway. Taking a deep breath, I started toward the garage, but then stopped once Paxton's phone began to ring. He refused to answer his calls, so I'd been carrying it around. And I definitely wasn't expecting to see Kyle's name pop up on the screen. Should I answer it or not? I hated him, but he *did* help us find out Rage's real name.

"Hello," I answered. The line went silent. "Kyle, it's Gabby, I know it's you."

"I wasn't expecting you to answer the phone," he replied.

"Paxton isn't doing much talking these days, so I've been answering his calls."

"Is he okay? I've been watching the news reports. I wanted to call and see how you guys were doing."

"Really?" I asked incredulously.

He sighed. "Believe it or not, I care. Paxton was my friend at one point or another. And right now, I have none. He reached out to me and now I'm reaching out to him."

I scoffed. "He's got a good life right now and he doesn't need all the bullshit you bring."

"I'm not trying to do shit to him," Kyle growled. "If you haven't heard, I can't exactly get into much trouble from a fucking wheelchair. I'm sorry for what I did to you and your family, but there's nothing I can do about that now. It's done. All I'm asking is for you to tell Pax that I called to ask about him. I'm trying to make things right."

It was strange hearing Kyle sound sincere. I even pulled the phone away from my ear to confirm that the screen still said it was him.

"Again, I'm sorry," he repeated and let out a heavy sigh. "Tell Pax I'll talk to him later."

"Wait, hold on," I grumbled. "It's kind of hard to talk to you and not be a bitch."

"I know and you don't have to explain. I'm kind of used to it by now."

"Have you talked to Kacey?" I asked curiously. After what he did to her, I was pretty sure she bitched him out every time he tried to talk to her.

"Not really," he confessed. "She won't talk to me. I've tried, but it's not like I can drive to her house and see her."

"True, but what you did was really fucked up. I was with her after it happened."

The line went quiet, but then his voice dipped low. "Thank you for helping her. I would give anything to take that night back."

"What's done is done, right? All we can do now is make up for our mistakes and do the right thing. If you're sincere in making amends, she'll come around one day."

"I doubt it," he added. "I fucked up and I know she'll never forgive me."

"You just have to keep trying." Which was what I needed to do with Paxton. I had to keep trying to talk to him until he let go of his fears.

"Thanks, Gabriella. I guess I never thought you'd ever talk to me. It surprised me."

A small smile splayed across my lips. "I'm glad I could surprise you. And don't worry, I'll tell Pax you called. I'm going to try and talk to him. Hopefully, he'll come around."

"He'd be stupid if he didn't."

After we said our goodbyes, I headed toward the garage and stood by the door. His hands were covered in grease and so were his T-shirt and jeans. He hadn't noticed me yet, but when I walked in, his body stiffened. I had to keep reminding myself what Mason just told me. But it was hard to push forward, when all I felt was rejection.

Without speaking, I came up behind him and wrapped my arms around his waist. "I'm not going anywhere," I promised. "If you need this time to yourself, that's fine, but I don't want you to shut me out when I know you need me. Please, just talk to me." Resting my forehead against his back, I broke down and cried. For the first time in my life, I sobbed without holding back, letting the tears come freely. When Paxton's hands closed over mine, I let go even more.

"I've missed you," he murmured. Taking my hands, he pulled them away from his body and pulled me around to his front. I placed them on my face and a smile splayed across his lips. "You realize I have grease all over me, don't you?"

I stared up into his sea green eyes and melted. "I don't care. As long as you're talking to me, nothing else matters. Whatever you're afraid of, you have to talk to me about it. I'm here to listen, always."

Hanging his head, he looked down at my hand and at the ring still on my finger. "I didn't mean to shut you out, Gabby. I was afraid to look you in the eyes and see nothing but disgust looking back at me. That was something I knew I wasn't ready to handle."

Grasping his shirt, I balled it up in my fists. "No, Paxton, that's not how I feel at all. I love you for who you are. If I had the chance to kill Rage, I would've done it and not thought twice. Think of all the women, including myself, you helped save. So, no, there will never be anything but love in my eyes for you. That I can promise."

Eyes glistening, he lowered his lips to mine and pressed down firmly. "I have a lot to make up for don't I?"

I smirked and ran my fingers through his hair. "Two and a half days, to be exact."

His gaze turned heated. Ripping off my shirt and pants, he slammed me down on the hood of his car, spreading me wide. "Well then, there's no time to waste."

EPILOGUE

Paxton
Fight Night

A MONTH HAD passed and things had slowly started to quiet down. Some people called me a murderer, some called me a saint. Of course, there were a handful of fighters who thought I should have to forfeit my title, but the league wasn't having any of that. As long as Gabriella was by my side, I didn't give a shit what anyone else said about me.

"Does she know about the party tonight?" Matt asked.

I knew Gabriella and Matt didn't have the best childhood as far as Christmas went. Their Christmas trees consisted of a small plastic one that could only hold a couple of ornaments. Not this year. It was our first Christmas together and I was going to make sure it was something she'd remember forever.

"No, she has no clue, but she's ecstatic to have Ryley and Ashleigh in town." Speaking of Ashleigh, they were off in the corner talking away when she should really be stretching. Now that Gabby and I lived together, I had permanently taken on the role as one of her coaches. Matt seemed to be pleased with her progress. She was ready for her fight. "I told everyone to give us an hour, so I can get her home and ready."

"And you don't think she'll mind that you invited Kacey and Tyler?"

Gabriella could be a jealous person at times, but I knew there was nothing to worry about with her and Tyler and vice versa with me and Kacey. Gabriella actually wanted to find a way to talk to Kacey about Kyle. I never thought the day would come when Gabby would feel bad for him.

About that time, Garrett Wells stormed through the door, out of breath; his suit and tie in disarray. "Holy shit, it's insane out there. Have you seen the amount of people?"

Gabby froze, eyes wide.

"Nice, Garrett. Good way to make her nervous," Matt scolded.

"No, on the contrary," she replied, "it's fucking *awesome*." We had trained vigorously for the past month and studied Allie's movements. She was more than ready.

"Just make sure you concentrate. We all know how you get when you're excited," Ryley stated.

Gabby rolled her eyes and punched him in the arm. "Trust me, I'm gonna concentrate. Have you seen my coaches? They'll kick my ass if I do something wrong."

She looked over at me and winked.

"Well, let's just hope you don't do anything wrong," Garrett said. Then he looked at his watch. "But right now we need to go. You'll be up soon."

Opening the door, Garrett walked out with Ryley and Ashleigh, leaving me and Matt with Gabby. We were both going to walk her down the aisle to the ring. "You can do this, Gabby," Matt told her. "You've gotten so much better. It must be all of that underground fighting."

"Or, it could be that I have two amazing coaches. I'll admit, Paxton's fighting is a lot different from yours." Standing up on her tiptoes, she kissed my cheek and smiled at her brother. "But it's what's going to help me win." Taking a deep breath, she turned toward the door. "All right you two. Let's go."

As soon as we left the room, camera flashes blinded us. Dressed in her red sports bra and black shorts, Gabby looked fiercer than I'd ever seen before. I had never been with a woman who could challenge me the way she does. Not to mention, she was hot as hell when she kicked ass in the ring.

"Remember, that's my sister you're looking at," Matt mumbled under his breath. When I looked over at him, a smirk splayed across his face. "It's going to take some getting used to, but I'm working on it."

"Don't worry, Reynolds. She's in good hands. Just remember, one day I'm going to be your brother-in-law."

"True enough. But if you so much as hurt her, I'm going to kick your ass. You got that?"

"Noted," I laughed. "But you don't have to worry about that." As far as everyone believed, Gabby and I were still engaged. After the party tonight, I was going to make it official.

"You know I can hear you, right?" Gabriella chuckled. We made it to the curtain just in time for the announcer to call Allie out. The crowd boomed with thunderous cheers, but it didn't seem to sway Gabby one bit. One thing we worked on pretty diligently was her focus. She was a master at it now, so I wasn't worried.

"And now, competing for the Bantamweight title championship is *Gabriella . . . The Machine . . . Reee-yyynnnooolllldddsss.*"

She looked back at me and Matt and winked. "Let's go boys."

The music blared overhead and the crowd went wild, her name echoing off the walls. Allie bounced on her feet in the ring, ready. When Gabriella hopped into the ring, the whole room sparked with energy. Both women smiled at each other and touched gloves before getting into position. Allie was one of the genuine fighters, like Mason, Matt, and Tyler. She wanted this fight to push herself, to compete against the best available. Gabby was definitely one of the best and she was going to show the world that tonight.

Ding, ding, ding. The fight was on.

Gabriella

ALLIE WAS ONE tough bitch. I saw stars when she punched me on the side of the face. However, that didn't stop me. One thing I was definitely good at was my floor game. My brother and Pax were experts. As soon as I got her down on the mat, it was game over. The second I felt her gloved hand tap on my arm, I let her go. She slumped over, hanging her head and instead of parading around the ring, I helped her up.

"I'm going to admit, I was scared shitless of fighting against you tonight," I confessed.

After catching her breath, she laughed and put her arm around me. "I'm not going to lie either. You thoroughly kicked my ass."

Smiling, I rubbed my sore jaw. "Don't worry, I'm going to have a sore face for quite a while."

We both laughed and bumped fists. "Merry Christmas, Reynolds. But don't get used to that title. I'm going to try and get it back."

"And I look forward to it." I winked at her and then rushed over to Paxton who had his arms outstretched. Jumping into them, I squealed and held on tight as he swung me around. "I did it," I shouted.

He set me down and the announcer came over and lifted my arm. "Ladies and gentlemen, I'd like to announce the new women's Bantamweight Champion, *Gabriella . . . The Machine . . . Reeeyyynnnooollldddsss.*"

The crowd went nuts, especially when Paxton and my brother lifted me up on their shoulders. It was surreal. I loved being a fighter, but I never thought I would be a title champion so fast in my career. It was a dream come true and definitely the best Christmas present ever.

"All right, sunshine, I'm ready to get you home."

Setting me down, I flung my arms around his neck and kissed him. "Oh yeah, I think I'm down for that."

"Okay, I think that's my cue to go." Matt squeezed my arm and kissed the side of my head. "You did great, sis. I'm so proud of you. I'll see you on Christmas and we'll celebrate with the family."

We all started out of the ring with my brother going one way and Paxton and I headed for the back. At every corner, there were people waiting for my autograph and picture. It was an amazing feeling. I'd watched my brother through the years, signing things and getting his picture taken, but never did I think it would happen to me.

After the last picture was snapped, Paxton rushed me to my room and grabbed my bag. I was so high off the excitement of my win, I didn't want the feeling to stop. I wanted the night to last forever and I sure as hell was going to celebrate. As soon as I got Paxton home, I knew exactly what I wanted to do.

The house was dark when we pulled up and even when we got inside, Paxton refused to turn on any lights. "What are you doing? Why can't we turn on the lights?" I asked.

Paxton's deep chuckle made me shiver. "You don't need to worry about that. Right now, you need to get in the shower."

"Are you going to join me?"

I followed him up the steps and into our room where he set my bag down. When he turned around, I noticed his cock bulging underneath his jeans. Holy hell, I wanted him. My clit throbbed with the need to feel him inside me. With all the excitement and adrenaline coursing through my veins, I didn't just want him to fuck me hard, I needed it.

Paxton sighed and rubbed his length through his jeans. "If you want me it's got to be fast. I need you showered and dressed in forty minutes."

By the mischievous gleam in his eyes, he had something planned. I could play along. "Fast, huh? I think I can handle that. I haven't been thoroughly fucked today." And right then, he pounced. One minute my shirt was on and the next it was on the floor along with my bra. His lips found a taut nipple and he bit, sucking it as hard as he could. Lifting me in his arms, he carried me into the bathroom and turned on the shower water, all while keeping his mouth on my breast.

Once the bathroom started to steam, he set me down and I unbuttoned my jeans, letting them fall to the floor. Paxton wasted no time shedding his clothes. As soon as we were both naked, he opened the shower door and pushed me inside. Lifting me up, he maneuvered his arms under my knees and I held on around his neck for dear life. Then he slammed his cock between my legs, and I cried out as my body bounced achingly hard up and down his length.

"Is this what you wanted? For me to fuck you hard?"

"Yes," I moaned breathlessly.

Lifting me off his cock, he set me down and turned me around. Pushing my shoulders down and into the shower wall, he spread me wide and lined himself up at my entrance. "Then brace yourself, sunshine. It's about to get harder."

The moment he thrust inside, I clenched him hard and screamed. Reaching around to my front, he fondled my clit with one hand and squeezed a breast with the other.

"You are so fucking tight," he growled. Our bodies slapped together and his relentless pace across my clit drove me insane. Clenching him tight, I climaxed. My body milked his cock and brought him to his release. Breathing hard, I leaned against the shower wall to catch my breath, not expecting Paxton to pull out of me so fast.

"What's the hurry?" I complained.

He slapped my ass and rinsed off. "Hurry up and you'll find out. Oh yeah, and wear your hair up."

By the time I turned around he was already exiting the shower. "Paxton, what's going on?"

Chuckling, he dried off and smiled. "You'll see."

After he shut the door, I rushed to finish washing up and hopped out. The moment I stepped into the bedroom, it was no longer dark. Lights twinkled from the hallway, giving our bedroom a glow, and on the bed there was a red dress and a letter.

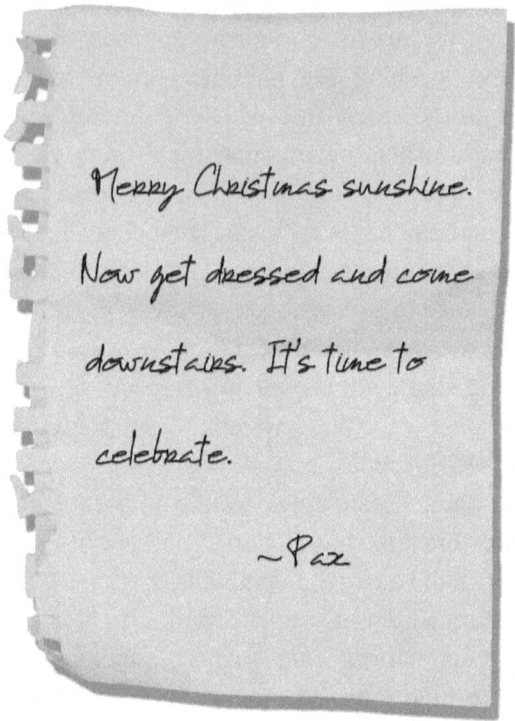

Merry Christmas sunshine. Now get dressed and come downstairs. It's time to celebrate.

~Pax

The dress was gorgeous with its flowing skirt and jeweled halter top. It sparkled just like the lights coming from the hallway. I heard voices coming from downstairs, along with the soft sound of Christmas music. As fast as I could, I put on my makeup and halfway dried my hair so I could throw it up in a classy updo. As more voices sounded from below, I quickly put on my dress with a pair of red heels. *What was going on?*

I gasped when I left the bedroom. Eyes wide, I couldn't believe what I was seeing. No wonder Paxton wanted it dark when we got back. The whole place was decorated for Christmas. Garland with white twinkling lights draped down the banisters and more lights shone from the living room down below. The voices were louder and once I was able to look down, the whole room was filled with my friends laughter and smiling faces. Not to mention, there was an eight foot Christmas tree in the middle of the room, surrounded by dozens of presents. It was breathtaking.

"Oh my God," I cried, slapping a hand over my mouth.

Ashleigh waved up at me and laughed. "Come on girl, it's time to party. I came all this way to see you and I don't want to waste a minute of it. Not only do we get to celebrate Christmas and your birthday, but also your new title."

Hot tears fell down my cheeks and when I turned around, Paxton was right there.

"Do you like it?" he asked.

"Are you kidding? This is amazing. I've never had a Christmas or birthday like this. Not with my friends and family all together. How did you know?"

Smile gone, he reached for my hands and pulled me to him. "Matt told me you two didn't have this growing up. I wanted to give you something special. And since you won the fight tonight, we have a lot more to celebrate." He kissed me and then led me down the stairs. Everyone I could ever hope to see was there. My mother was talking to Paxton's Aunt and Uncle, while April and her son played with my nephew. Matt and Shelby waved at me and so did Tyler and Kacey.

After I waved, I looked up at Paxton. "I'm surprised you invited them."

He shrugged. "I didn't think you'd mind. Besides, I remember you telling me about wanting to talk to Kacey."

"I do. I also wanted to speak with Ryley. Have you by any chance talked to Camden?"

"Not since he left town. I wonder how long he'll stay gone?" That was a good question.

"I'm not sure. However, if there's one thing I do know, it's that it's Christmas and we all need forgiveness in our lives. I'll be right back." Paxton chuckled because he knew what my mission was. If I could forgive Kyle, of all people, then hope wasn't lost on the others.

Ryley held out his arms when I approached and I walked into them. "Good fight tonight, Gabby."

"Thanks," I replied. Ashleigh glowed just like every young mother does when they're carrying a child. In this case, it would be two . . . a boy and a girl. "I have a question," I said to them both. Ryley took a sip of his beer and lifted his brows. "Have you talked to Camden?"

Ashleigh pursed her lips and Ryley hung his head. "No, why would I have talked to him? He left town, remember?"

"I know, but I honestly think he needs help. If you by any chance come in contact with him, please remember that he helped save me. If it wasn't for him, I don't know if I'd be here right now."

Ryley sighed. "I know. It's just hard to forgive him for the things he's done. But if he does happen to call, I'll talk to him. I can't promise anything beyond that."

Breathing a sigh of relief, I smiled and hugged him tight. "That's all I ask. I'm making my rounds of forgiveness tonight."

"At least you don't have to match make," Ashleigh

teased.

"Yes, I know. You two about killed me." Tyler and Kacey were in the corner; they were my next stop. "All right, now on to my next mission."

"Oh, goodness," Ashleigh chuckled as I walked away.

Both Tyler and Kacey smiled at me when I waltzed up, and thankfully, Paxton joined me. "I'll keep Tyler busy while you talk to Kacey," he whispered in my ear.

He was a life saver. "Thank you."

While Paxton started a conversation with Tyler, I politely cut in and stole Kacey's attention. "Can I talk to you for a minute?" Furrowing her brows, she nodded and reluctantly stepped away. "How are you? Is the restaurant going okay?"

Her face beamed. "The restaurant is amazing. It's taken off so fast."

"That's good," I remarked with a smile. "Now that things have calmed down here, I'm hoping Paxton and I can take a trip out there. I could always use some good food."

"Well, I'd be glad to have you both. It's nice seeing him happy again."

"And what about you? Have you talked to Kyle?"

Her smile faded. "No. He's tried calling, but I'm just not ready to speak to him yet."

After all she'd been through, I couldn't argue. "I totally understand. But I wanted to tell you something that I don't think you know."

"What do you mean?"

Taking a deep breath, I let it out and just said it. "I talked to him."

Her eyes went wide. "What? Why would you do

that?"

"It was pretty dicey at first. I had so much hatred built up, it was hard to see he was trying to help us. Once I got past the anger, I could actually hear the regret in his voice," I trailed off. "But I'm getting off track. I thought you should know that he helped us figure out who Rage was. He was the one who gave us his real name."

"Really?" she asked incredulously. "I guess I can't see him doing that, not unless he'd gain something in return."

"So far he hasn't asked for anything. The last time I talked to him, he sounded really messed up. I think he misses you. And with being alone at Christmas, I know it can't be easy."

Her eyes misted over and the tears fell. "Thanks for the information, Gabriella. It's nice to know that he might be coming around. I'll call him for Christmas, but I'm not going to forgive him. It's going to take a lot more than that."

"I understand. I just wanted you to know."

She smiled through her tears and walked back to Tyler, who had been watching on curiously. He wasn't going to like that I was talking to Kyle, but he'd eventually get over it.

"How did it go?" Paxton asked.

"As good as can be expected. I at least tried."

Taking my hand, he led me out the back door to the patio with a blanket tucked under his arm. The night was chilly and when I shivered, he put the blanket over my shoulders. "Let's take a walk."

Before stepping onto the sand, I slipped off my heels and followed beside him. "I can't thank you enough for having the party. This day has been phenomenal. I don't want it to end."

"It's not over yet." Paxton turned to me and took both of my hands in his. His fingers tenderly traced the ring on my finger. "I have a confession to make," he whispered, glancing down at my hand.

My pulse sped and I swallowed hard. He wasn't smiling, and it made me nervous. "What is it?"

His sea green gaze lifted to mine. "Do you remember the day I gave you the ring?"

How could I forget? I could recall every single word. "Yes, I remember it quite well," I answered.

Taking a deep breath, he let it out slowly. "Well, I'm here to tell you that everything I said was the truth. It might have been part of a ploy, but I meant every word I said. You have no idea how much I love seeing that ring on your finger. It lets everyone know that you're mine."

Tears filled my eyes. "That's why I never want to take it off."

His lips touched mine and then he pulled my bottom one between his teeth. "I hope you know what you're getting into. Now that I have you, I'm not going to let you go."

"Promise?"

"You better fucking believe it."

Camden's Redemption
(Coming Spring 2015)

ACKNOWLEDGMENTS

FIRST AND FOREMOST, I want to give a HUGE thank you to my readers. I will always and forever be grateful for the love and support that you show me. Without you nothing would be possible. Also, without my family and friends I wouldn't have such unique characters. Little do they know that I actually write about them. Shh . . . don't say anything. It's our secret. I have such an amazing team that I work with and I would be lost without them. My husband is one of the main ones. When I talk to him about ideas for future books, if he hates the idea then I know to go with it. I'm a rebel like that. :)

My PA is always there for my emotional support and I probably wouldn't have any hair on my head if it wasn't for her. Of course, my publicist has to put up with me too. Hopefully, she won't kick me to the curb one day. My editor is freaking awesome and has really made my fighters shine. I'm in awe of her talent. My cover designer is so talented I don't know how she does it. Also, if it wasn't for my formatter, the insides wouldn't look as cool as they do. I love how she makes it unique. Basically, I need to thank every single one of you who are reading this right now. This is me giving you *BIG HUGGLES.* You all rock!

ABOUT THE AUTHOR

NEW YORK TIMES and USA Today Bestselling author, L.P. Dover, is a southern belle residing in North Carolina along with her husband and two beautiful girls. Before she even began her literary journey she worked in Periodontics enjoying the wonderment of dental surgeries.

Not only does she love to write, but she loves to play tennis, go on mountain hikes, white water rafting, and you can't forget the passion for singing. Her two number one fans expect a concert each and every night before bedtime and those songs usually consist of Christmas carols.

Aside from being a wife and mother, L.P. Dover has written over nine novels including her Forever Fae series, the Second Chances series, and her standalone novel, *Love, Lies, and Deception*. Her favorite genre to read is romantic suspense and she also loves writing it. However, if she had to choose a setting to live in it would have to be with her faeries in the Land of the Fae.

L.P. Dover is represented by Marisa Corvisiero of Corvisiero Literary Agency.

OTHER BOOKS BY L.P. DOVER

Forever Fae Series

Second Chances Standalones

Gloves Off Series

Standalone (Romantic Suspense)

ALSO CHECK OUT THESE
EXTRAORDINARY AUTHORS & BOOKS:

Alivia Anders ~ Illumine
Cambria Hebert ~ Recalled
Angela Orlowski Peart ~ Forged by Greed
Julia Crane ~ Freak of Nature
J.A. Huss ~ Tragic
Cameo Renae ~ Hidden Wings
A.J. Bennett ~ Now or Never
Tabatha Vargo ~ Playing Patience
Beth Balmanno ~ Set in Stone
Ella James ~ Selling Scarlett
Tara West ~ Visions of the Witch
Heidi McLaughlin ~ Forever Your Girl
Melissa Andrea ~ The Edge of Darkness
Komal Kant ~ Falling for Hadie
Melissa Pearl ~ Golden Blood
Alexia Purdy ~ Breathe Me
Sarah M. Ross ~ Inhale, Exhale
Brina Courtney ~ Reveal
Amber Garza ~ Falling to Pieces
Anna Cruise ~ Maverick